PEOPLE WANT TO LIVE

McSWEENEY'S
SAN FRANCISCO

Versions of some stories in this book first appeared in the following: "Heroes" in *Colorado Review*; "Bulletproof Bus" in *J Journal*; "Tourism" in the *Southern Review*; "Foreigners" in *Ecotone*; "Loved Ones" in *The Arkansas International*; "Believers" in *Shenandoah*; "The Effect of Heat on Poor People" in *Kenyon Review Online*; "Together" as "Close Together" in *Room*; "Present Tense" in *Copper Nickel*; "The Leavers" as "Exit for the Faithful" in *Bellevue Literary Review*.

McSweeney's and colophon are registered trademarks of McSweeney's, an independent publisher based in San Francisco.

ISBN: 978-1-952119-29-3

Cover illustration by Sunra Thompson

10   9   8   7   6   5   4   3   2   1

www.mcsweeneys.net

Printed in the United States

PEOPLE
WANT
TO LIVE

STORIES

FARAH ALI

McSWEENEY'S

SAN FRANCISCO

For my parents and my brother

HEROES

A WEEK AFTER THEIR son had been shot dead in a street, Salma and Asaf sat staring at each other across the big white sheet on the floor of their drawing room. On one end was a pile of prayer beads and on the other end stood two low tables with a few books of prayers on them, each book the size of an adult's palm. The center of the sheet was rumpled and made Salma think of the people who had sat here in turns, all week long, marking their spots in invisible ways. It was time to fold the sheet and take it to the dry cleaner.

When the last wave of visitors had left, shuffling out of the gate to their cars, heads bowed in a gesture meant to convey respect, Salma felt intensely jealous. They would be able to hug their sons and daughters, look at them more intently and not find fault with them—at least for a few days. Now Salma's house was so quiet. Their daughter Sophia was somewhere, probably in her room. They should see if she was hungry; there must be tea and biscuits for her to eat. But first, this quiet. Maybe the murmurs of the condolence-givers had been a necessary filler after all.

It was a strange thing to discover about one's self, she thought, to be surprised by new lows in one's character. She had always assumed that if ever faced with a problem of a catastrophic nature, she would be the one to handle it with grace and foresight, helping a blundering Asaf. The opposite turned out to be true. But then, even in her wildest assumptions, she had never thought that her son would be dead at fifteen.

She disliked having to put away her own feelings to make room for the sadness of others. All these people had entered her home and occupied spaces that Jamaal used to sit on or stand on or leave his shoes on. Her husband's mother had rushed into the house, her hair coming out of its bun, as if sudden tragedy demanded unkemptness. His sisters had lurched in, mouths agape, their children and spouses entering more grimly. When they'd come in, they had looked around wildly for the arms of loved ones to catch them, but Salma had not moved from her place, nor smiled or cried or said words of comfort. Her parents had been the last to arrive that day. They had taken the first available flight to Karachi from Rawalpindi. They had stood at her door and said, in voices trembling with emotion and age, "You have lost a son, but you still have your old parents, by the grace of God."

"I hate them," Salma said later, with vigor. "Especially the parents of Jamaal's friends. Did you see the relief in their eyes?" The mothers hugged her, the fathers patted her husband on the back. They murmured soft words, dabbed their eyes. And Salma knew what they thought, *Thank God it wasn't him*. Or *her*. Or *them*. She spoke only to answer questions. Asaf was better at this than she was. Salma wanted to stop opening the door when the bell rang. But the neighbors and the relatives and the friends kept trickling in, and she watched her parents greet them all, and serve them tea and kebabs and vanilla tea cake from the bakery. "All we can do is have patience. Sabar," the visitors said, and her parents nodded and murmured, "He went too soon." Back and forth, a seesaw of endless lament.

It irritated Salma, this assumption on her parents' part that they understood; their lives had been unburdened with illnesses or untimely deaths. She was still here, wasn't she? How she hated that. Her mother misunderstood the look on her face. "We are not going anywhere," she said one afternoon, reassurance and patience in her voice. "Don't you worry, beti." Salma did not want them to be here, but it would have made her seem completely unhinged had she said that out loud.

Every evening, her parents talked about Jamaal while Asaf's parents listened, and Asaf added his own words to their descriptions of him. So, in Salma's mind, Jamaal became taller ("he had been tall for his age"), kinder ("remember when he helped his cousin with his homework"), a model son ("he never talked back, was always responsible"). But the last phrase resisted being pinned onto the glorious monument that was building in her memory. Once he had shouted at her, his face red and his voice straining as he told her to leave his room.

It was terrible that they had to resume eating and drinking and sleeping. Now they sat at the dining table for breakfast, having ordinary toast and eggs and drinking ordinary tea. The sounds of TV and Jamaal were missing. It was always going to be this way now. Salma imagined a whole series of forevers climbing up her like a vine, the *r* of one linked to the *f* of the other, choking her.

"I have to go back to work," said Asaf, and Sophia added, "I should go back to school," and Salma realized that it would be wonderful to not have to see them for a while. Then she felt guilty because what she should have been doing, what she should at least have been *wanting* to do, was grab Sophia and hug her and not let her go to school.

Someone had foolishly said to her, "You still have your daughter." Asaf was saying something now and she made herself pay attention to it. "It will do you good when you go back to teaching," he said.

She supposed it was time now for everyone to want to feel some relief, and to move on to other routines and faces. Her parents returned to Rawalpindi and Asaf to his office. Sophia and Salma entered the school together, and, wordlessly, they split. Jamaal's friends were here somewhere. Salma would not look for them, she decided. For a moment, she felt a little lost. Asaf was probably already creating lists of things to do, and Sophia was working hard at not remembering her brother's presence in the school's grounds and corridors. Salma opened the folder which contained lesson plans for English Literature. Jamaal would have been one of her students this year.

The staffroom at the school was Salma's least favorite place. The arrangement of the sofas left no room for one's own thoughts; one's face was always presented for scrutiny to the person sitting across the room. "At least he died when he was still an innocent child," said a teacher who liked to think that she was a special friend of Salma's during this difficult time. Her words made Salma's mouth go thin; she wanted to growl at the woman. Another time, a different well-intentioned teacher said, "You must not let yourself become morbid." He taught history and was used to dead things.

The school principal had a talk with Salma, of course. Was the family thinking of a commemorative plaque, a grant, his name on a bench? Salma shook her head. The lady who had taught Jamaal Urdu three years ago reminded her in urgent, soft tones that the boy had been her brightest and most respectful student. Here again, a piece of truth broke free; Salma remembered a day when she had cried in frustration because Jamaal had failed another test in school and had looked unmoved.

It was a new kind of normal to get used to. Sophia and Salma came home together when the school day ended and had a late lunch. In the evening, they had small cakes with fondant icing. Sometimes Salma asked her daughter about school and her friends, and Sophia answered in as few words as possible. One such time, Salma looked at her and told her that she did not have to stay at the table if it made her uncomfortable. Her daughter took a deep breath and continued eating her cake.

For a while, Salma fell into the habit of counting how often the phrases "tragic incident" and "brave survivors" appeared in newspapers to summarize that day. She paused images on TV, morning and night, cut out Jamaal's detailed obituaries in one or two leading publications. She saved all the articles and showed them to Asaf. When the newspapers moved on to other things, Salma told Asaf that they should sell their house and move to Lahore. She was surprised when he agreed. A new place, a new house, a new supermarket, and new roads to understand and own. To get the metallic taste of Karachi out of their mouths.

"There are more trees there," Salma said, lying in bed at night.

"They get proper winter. We'll need jackets. And sweaters, and maybe gloves." Asaf loved winter.

"We'll find a place with trees."

"It shouldn't be a problem getting a new house in Lahore."

"How do you feel about this? Would you be OK with this?" they asked Sophia, sharing a strange feeling of excitement. She was, after all, sixteen.

"I don't care," she said.

Salma felt disappointed. She had been expecting a fight or, at the very least, a prolonged argument. She lost her sense of urgency after that, but Asaf started looking for work in Lahore. Salma watched him as he sat with his laptop, typing and browsing and clicking furiously. His face started to remind her of Jamaal, so she stopped watching him. She remembered how, when Jamaal was born, Asaf's family had said that the baby looked *nothing* like his mother and *completely* like his father. In a postpartum daze, Salma had looked at her baby's closed, crusted-over eyes and lightly yellowed skin and wondered where in the world they saw the likeness. Now, sitting on the sofa hearing her husband type away, she felt angry that her in-laws had willed the resemblance upon her son. And she realized, suddenly, *We're going to leave Jamaal in this city.*

When the season turned cooler, Salma rolled up her sleeves and went into Jamaal's room. She opened the doors of his cupboard and, one by one, took out his shirts and shorts and pants and folded them. Sometimes her heart beat fast, sometimes her hands trembled. She experimentally sniffed a shirt but did not feel anything. She packed his things into suitcases and gave them to her maasi, the woman who came to her house every morning to mop the floors and wash the dishes. The maasi had a moment of doubt before accepting such a generous donation—did she really want her own sons wearing the clothes of a dead boy? Her hesitation was only for a few seconds though, and, grabbing Salma's hands with her callused ones, she called for God's wrath upon the heads of the killers.

"I gave away his clothes today. All of them," she told her husband that night. Asaf's lips trembled and he wiped his eyes, and Salma felt powerful and stubborn and in control of herself. Asaf said it was a heartless thing to do, but right away he apologized for saying that. But Salma was already feeling sad and mean; it was wrong of her to not have kept every last dirty sock.

She began to fill the room with expletives. Asaf pleaded with her to be quiet, then he put on a song on his laptop and turned the volume up as high as it could go. He sat with his knees drawn up while the song played and his wife shouted.

The next morning, Salma woke up and saw Asaf looking at her tentatively, as if conducting a silent assessment of her emotional state. Salma's insides were always going to be a little bruised now, but she smiled at Asaf to show that she had turned a corner. She told him that today she was going to complete cleaning up Jamaal's room.

She took off the sheets her son had last slept on, and then she started pulling the mattress off the bed. *No room for him in a new house*, she made herself think briskly, her teeth biting her tongue in painful fortitude. The mattress tumbled to the floor. Taped to the side that had rested on the slats was a small, rectangular plastic packet. Salma peeled it off and looked inside it: small round pills with hearts and smiley faces on them. She made a sound that was between a surprised "oh" and a calm "ah." Clutching the bag, she walked swiftly to her room. "Ecstasy," her browser's search engine declared after she typed in a description. She didn't know what to make of this. She paced her room in anger, breathing hard, putting away clothes and straightening the bed, the bag in her fist. She thought, *Should they ground him or kick him out of the house?* She had never seen him use the drugs. She wanted to say, "It's those friends of his," but the tenses of her thoughts were confusing her. Nothing was easy to understand anymore. She went back to her son's room.

She sat down on the mattress and wondered about other things—if her parents needed any money, if her students wanted to put up a play this year—until Asaf came home and Jamaal's glow-in-the-dark clock told her it was eight o'clock.

She put the plastic packet inside a zippered space in her handbag and ate dinner with her family. She tried to keep her voice free of clues as she talked to Asaf. She glanced at Sophia and wondered if she had known. Had Jamaal and Sophia been friendly, secret-sharing siblings? She tried to be shrewd about the past, tried to remember her children's behavior and expressions and statements, but nothing came to mind.

They could not have been Jamaal's, she thought in bed later. Her thoughts, as she sank into sleep, were the very clichés she urged her students to avoid.

The bag and what it contained became a dangerous, coveted object to Salma. She kept it by her side as much as she could. On Monday, she taught her class while the bag stayed on the floor next to her chair. The children worked quietly and she felt a momentary pain in her head which she knew was only because this was a room full of her son's friends but not him. There was the chair Jamaal might have sat on, exchanging nervous glances with his friends who shared his terrible secret. "Damn! My own *mom* is here, teaching Shakespeare, and she doesn't know!" he might have said and then they would have high-fived at the sheer daring of it all. He might have hated being taught by his mother, but she would have liked to teach him English Literature. He had liked words, working with them in sentences, looking up meanings. He had written wonderful essays. *He was a good boy who had been misled by the wrong company he had kept*, thought Salma. Hadn't she sized up those parents in a glance at parent-teacher meetings? Their children left to drivers and maids, no one to check them. Feeling angry numbed her temporarily.

The cold, logical part of her mind, though, kept realigning the facts around Jamaal's death: he hadn't died because of who he was or what he was consuming. The police had informed them that Jamaal's wallet and mobile phone had not been found on or near his body, and it was assumed that the killers had taken them after they had put the bullets in. *Give and take.*

Salma's eyes felt itchy with dryness. When she went home that day, she picked up all the newspapers from her bedside table, her bed, the room where the TV was, and made a pile of them for the man who came by with his cart to collect them.

She emptied the fridge and cleaned the shelves and threw away the vegetables that had rotted. She shook her head at her carelessness. She'd taught her children it was wrong to waste food. She dusted the neglected places on window ledges and the metal flower embellishment on the front gate. It was important to look clean.

———

It came to her attention that people spoke to her softly, as if she were terminally ill. The old uncle who ran the grocery store in her neighborhood, the chowkidaar who guarded their street at night, the attendants at the petrol station, the people in the bank. *How did they all know?* She reveled in their kind consideration, real or otherwise. If in a long line at the supermarket, she imagined tapping the shoulder in front of her and saying, "Excuse me. My son was killed. Can I go first?" And if they said no, she would say, "He was murdered." But what if they responded, "You know, he was just an addict, a charsi." Then she would have to run out of there with her hands over her ears. She would still hear them shouting, "What kind of a mother are you anyway?"

———

Asaf wanted to go through old pictures on his laptop. He brought out a tub of chocolate ice cream and bowls and spoons. Sophia, who rarely said no to him, sat with her arms folded. Salma sat down as well, willing to go along with it. She felt guilty for not sharing with Asaf that very important fact about Jamaal, who had been *their* son after all. Not just hers. She felt even worse when she saw the embarrassingly desperate look of yearning on her husband's face as he clicked on picture after picture. There was Jamaal when he was just born, then one, then two. Minutes passed, and now he was fifteen. Salma looked hard at the image of his face. He was sitting with them on a sofa wearing Eid clothes. His smile was lopsided, almost cynical. And here he was eating ice cream on a winter night, not smiling. *Had he disliked his shirt or his ice cream?* Salma wondered. Asaf's fingers touched the screen. "He looks so happy," he said. Sophia had sunk back into the sofa but her eyes had not left the screen. Now she got up and broke the spell. The ice cream was a puddle in its container.

Salma knew what she needed. Inside the bathroom, she opened her bag and looked at the array of pills. Three yellow ones with smiley faces, two pink ones with hearts, and two plain blue ones. They were all there, as Jamaal had last seen them. *Which one would my boy have pulled out next?* Would he have shown disdain toward the ones with the hearts? She felt sad that he hadn't been comfortable sharing this secret with his mother while he was alive.

"He liked writing essays and sometimes poems. He'd been trying to finish a story," the English-language daily reporter had noted when he called about the obituary. He had changed all her tenses from present to past. She worried that they would misspell his name, put one *a* instead of two. But his name, the entire paragraph, in fact, had no errors. "Jamaal means beauty," Salma wanted to tell the reporter, but had felt embarrassed about saying it. Instead, she had said, "He was a good boy."

———————

Six months after Jamaal had been killed, his parents and sister were invited to a discussion on a morning talk show on TV about violence and the families left behind. Sophia refused to go, but Asaf and Salma went and sat nervously and were assured by the hostess that they did not have to talk about things in detail. Their faces looked pale in the colorful surroundings. Asaf spoke movingly, haltingly, about their bright, beautiful boy. But Salma knew that Jamaal wasn't beautiful or ugly, exceptionally kind or cruel. He was average, and he had stopped going outside to play cricket and stopped joking with his sister and had become unkind to his mother. She had thought he was just being a moody teenager. Now, of course, she knew better. Better than her husband knew his son, she realized, and felt pleased for a moment.

Asaf watched the show and recorded it. Salma heard him play it over and over again. After the fourth time, he said to her, "We must move," his eyes extra large and bright.

In early spring, Asaf flew to Lahore for a job interview. In the car on the way to the airport, Salma worried out loud about loneliness and the house being too quiet, and were they really going to move? She spoke fast because she felt bad. *What if Asaf's plane crashed and he died not knowing?* At the airport, he said to his daughter, "Take care of your mother." Salma cringed. *Taking care* was not the kind of thing that Sophia did.

In the night, she read, again, about the symptoms and signs of ecstasy users. The list was familiar to her by now, but it was hard trying to get a true, clear picture of Jamaal's features in her mind. That last day he had looked so happy. That is what she had always thought; it had been such a relief to her to see him smiling. He said that he'd be back soon, and she had thought it wiser not to ask where he was going or with whom.

Asaf called her from Lahore.

"After they confirm my job," he said, "we can move in two weeks. I've looked around a few places here. There's one house that I like a lot. It's close to a mosque."

"Hm."

"Faith gives me sustenance. I'd be lost without it."

He could be articulate sometimes, just like their boy, who had won a debate once at the age of thirteen.

"I found this," Sophia said. Salma had asked for her help in going through Jamaal's things. They worked in different parts of his room. Sophia climbed over the mattress that lay on top of the curtains and the rug, and sat at her brother's table, opening and shutting drawers. Now she stood before Salma, not looking directly into her face, and held out a piece of white notebook paper.

Salma took the sheet and saw Jamaal's handwriting on it. Beautiful slopes and curves, not a dot out of place.

"I didn't know he could write in Urdu so well," Sophia said. Her voice was plain and even.

"It's a poem."

"It's only homework." Sophia paused, then added, "He wasn't the only one who died that day, you know."

Salma took a step back.

Sophia raised her voice. "He is not a martyr. The newspapers are wrong."

Salma put the paper with Jamaal's poem in her bag, next to the pills. Other memories slowly squeezed to the front of her brain: Jamaal sitting, staring at his homework in perplexity, and then tearing a book in half. His math teacher saying that Jamaal needed extra tutoring. The Urdu language teacher holding a whispered conference with her in the empty staffroom one sunny afternoon, asking her if she knew why Jamaal had fallen asleep in class two times now.

———

Then, one day, a video clip started going around on the internet. It was jerky and a little under a minute and shot from someone's cell phone. It showed a pair of men, their faces covered, guns in hands, moving with speed through a crowd. Salma searched through the screaming people for her son, but she could not find him. The men yelled words that might have been from an old movie about good versus evil, and then they shot their shots. She watched it by herself and then asked Asaf to watch it with her. He groaned and said, "How is Sophia going to study for her final exams now?"

"She has done really well," Sophia's teacher told Salma at the end of the term.

"She has always been a good student," Salma said flatly. There was no pride in her voice.

"A *most excellent* student." The teacher was quick to confirm the cleverness and bravery and strength of Sophia. Her sympathy was naked: poor Sophia, who lost a brother to violence; poor Salma, a mother who lost a son.

In June, Jamaal's and Sophia's friends decided to hold a small candlelight vigil at their school for him. They wanted to remember what had happened a year ago. The children invited their parents and other people to attend it, and Sophia invited her mother and her father. It was, it seemed to Salma when it ended, a new way to mourn. She had not wanted to go, but the idea of a vigil became popular at the school, and the teachers and the principal and the cleaners and the guards all decided that it was their duty to be a part of it. Solidarity. She went with Asaf and stood at the back, holding a candle and feeling alternately numb and stupid. The pills radiated heat from deep inside her bag. In the end, it had turned into a memorial for all the people who had died that day, and it was hard for Salma to find the rectangle of Jamaal's picture from among the others on the wall. Once she found it, she kept her eyes fastened to it. Somewhere in the front rows was Sophia, her face indistinguishable from her friends' faces in the candlelight. For those moments, Jamaal could have been anyone's brother. Later that night at home, Salma flushed Jamaal's pills and the poem down the toilet.

The newspapers wrote about the vigil. Again, they described what had happened on a street in Karachi twelve months ago. Journalists contacted those who had survived and pressed them to relive that afternoon. One man recalled, "A young boy pushed me to the ground and covered me." *Heroes*, the reporters called the victims and their families.

BULLETPROOF BUS

THE BULLETPROOF BUS GLIDES through the city. Potholes and pockmarked speed bumps don't bother it. It does not tear through red lights; instead, it slows down gracefully and gradually until it reaches a complete stop. Unlike other drivers with their buses, the bulletproof bus driver knows and understands the rules. He has Respect for the Law.

Sadaf is the first person I tell all this to. "I'm going to apply for the bus driver job," I say casually. She is nursing the baby and doesn't look up and chooses to stay quiet. So I go on pretending to read the newspaper and, after five minutes, she says, "What do you mean, bus driver job?"

The words in my mind stumble in their hurry to come out in an impressive, orderly way.

"It's that new bus, the bulletproof one. I heard they're looking for a driver, and the pay is good."

I sound like a fool. I glance at her face, but it's hard to look at the frown and the shadows under her eyes, so I go back to glancing at the newspaper. A fire, a robbery, a man who killed his children, and film awards. My heart is beating fast. What is her opinion about my idea? Does she believe in me?

She says, "What do you have to do to get the job?" And at those words, I feel as good as if I'd already achieved success. I tell her about the name of the man who owns this special bus, that there is no other like it in all of Karachi right now, that there are tourists who pay a lot of money to ride in the Karachi King Express. I tell her about the places the tourists go—Empress Market, Saint Patrick's Church, a Parsi temple, a Hindu temple.

Sadaf asks, intrigued, "What do they do there?"

I dig into details, adding and subtracting. "They take pictures and make videos. They tell others how great and misunderstood and underestimated our city is," I tell her. "They write about the wonderful history of Karachi, the forgotten places, the people who are the soul of the city." The last few lines I memorized from the ad in the newspaper. My friend Abid had read them to me because I can't read English very well and I'm not too proud to ask for help when I need it. Sadaf, worn out after cooking and taking care of the baby, doesn't mind asking me what on earth it all means. I start explaining but she interrupts me by getting up suddenly.

She frowns and says, "I don't think you're going to get the job. It sounds too difficult for you." While I'm still shrinking, she picks up the baby and goes into the other room, one of two in our shack.

I have been asking around for work ever since the juice seller fired me because he said I moved too slowly and cost him customers. But Hamza, who goes to a construction site every morning when it's still dark, wouldn't tell me the name of the man who got him the job. I suspect his mother's brother helped him. I don't want to ask Bilal because all he does is sell papar for twelve hours straight and comes home smelling of it. All day long, he walks from one end of Clifton Beach to another with a pole over his shoulders, bags of papar hanging on each side. When he complained about backache, I laughed. How heavy could crispy bread be? He said that after six months of carrying it, it could bend a man's shoulders. Then he thanked God so he wouldn't sound ungrateful because at least he was earning a decent amount. I wonder now if Sadaf wouldn't mind my shoulders getting misshapen if it meant steady money.

I haven't told anyone else about my plans to apply for the driver job. Someone with envy in his heart could give me the evil eye and who knows what might happen then. Chacha Fazal tells me that for all of the thirty years he had saved money to buy his own shop, he hadn't told a single soul, not even his wife or brothers. Especially not his brothers. Brothers can be dangerously envious. But I need to tell someone with experience, someone who can help me, because I don't know where to start. The next morning, I sit down to shave my face. Sadaf takes a look and rolls her eyes, but I ignore that and tell her in a crisp voice that I'm heading out for work in a little while.

Chacha Fazal's shop isn't busy, which is good and bad. Good because it means I can have a private conversation with him without the whole mohalla listening. Bad because the reeking mass of sodden plastic bags and their contents have been blocking the path to the shop for three weeks now and are the reason the place is empty. I have to lift the hems of my shalwar and ignore the wet sounds my shoes make as I walk over it. His smile welcomes me and I tell him I need his help. Chacha listens intently, stroking his white beard. He frowns in thoughtfulness. All these little actions fill me with confidence.

"I might be able to help you," he says. "A nephew of mine works as a driver in a bank."

I remember Chacha boasting about him. This, too, he had announced only after the nephew had worked there for a solid three months and his chances of being fired were minimal. Chacha is tremendously helpful; he writes down his nephew's number for me and I feel a twinge of guilt. A year ago, he had wanted me to marry his oldest daughter, but I'd already promised to marry Sadaf. Chacha had seemed to not mind. He'd also come to the wedding, and he eventually found someone for his daughter. But every now and then, I wonder if he doesn't secretly despise me. I make a note to send him some mithai in case I get the job.

I hadn't thought it would be so easy to get started. Already, things are moving fast, faster than I'd thought they would. I can't help picturing myself grasping the bus's steering wheel with one hand—no, two, because one is irresponsible—and maneuvering the rust-free, crack-free, all-parts-working body of the bulletproof bus along wide roads and narrow streets. I walk toward home as if I'm the owner of the King Express.

I want to buy something for Sadaf and even the baby, but, with a flash of reason, I don't because I only have the smallest amount of change left in my pocket and there is not much to go on until the job is mine. I haven't had any money coming in since the juice seller's and that was almost a month ago.

In the evening, I stop for tea at Yusuf's chai cart—he took it over from his father who died a few months ago. Two rupees for a cup of chai—Yusuf gives me a discount for the sake of friendship. Everyone knows I've been struggling to make ends meet for a while now. Jobs are hard to come by. It's busy at that hour, the men in the neighborhood coming home from work. I talk to them about things, but not about the bus. It's going to be better-paying work than what these men do and I remember Chacha's cautioning words about envy. I hope fervently that the old man keeps to himself all that I've told him.

A few days pass before I gather the courage to call the nephew. After three rings I wonder if I should cut the call and try again—if voicemail starts, I'll lose precious minutes from my balance. At that moment, someone says hello, and I stammer a hello then salaam. I ask for Mr. Uzair—the nephew—and the voice confirms that it is him. With each slow, practiced word that comes out of my mouth, my confidence goes down. To my ears, I whimper to an end. I want to tell him, "I just want a chance to drive the bulletproof bus." Instead, I wait for him to say something, to tell me that he can't help me. I admit to myself, shamefacedly, that I would be relieved to hear that. But Mr. Uzair is speaking. I press the phone to my ear.

He tells me that there is a Mr. Cheema who hires drivers for the Daewoo bus service—he might be able to help me out with Karachi King Express. In a daze, I add Mr. Cheema's number to the scrap of paper and that's the end of the call. I stand on the spot for a few minutes, savoring this feeling of easy progress. At that moment, I am convinced that, for a man, there is nothing worthier than honest hard work. I stand there and deliver a speech in my head about giving my job my best. I will memorize the names of the places on all the routes. I will improve my manners of greeting and talking with those more literate than me. I will always be shining clean.

Sadaf and the baby are not back yet from the market—bargaining always takes a long time, especially when you have to make a few rupees last and last. There is something I have been meaning to give her, and I take it out from where I've been hiding it. Today seems to be a good day to give it.

I have bought her a phone. She has never had one before—her first husband hadn't allowed it. This phone is white and thin, and I got it for a good price from Muhammad Moosa. I'd told him what I wanted and he'd said he knew someone and I'd have the phone in a week's time. He'd named a price and I'd brought it down and he'd agreed. When I went to get the cell phone, he started whining and lying about unexpected difficulties and said that the price had gone up. I asked him what his mother would say if she heard him, especially since she had named him after two prophets. He frowned at the mention of his mother and took the money I gave him.

Sadaf is tired and irritable when she gets home and seeing me there makes her more annoyed. "Don't you ever have any work to do?" she says.

I want to tell her about getting Mr. Cheema's number, but first I want to give her the phone. She gets busy right away, though, moving past me and around me until I go sit in a corner, out of her way. She bangs down a pot on the single burner and, with quick movements, fills it with whatever she's bought. Some moments later, I smell potatoes. I would have liked chicken, but she refuses to spend that much on food, saying that we'll deserve it when I've stuck to a job for longer than two months.

It is hard for me to keep sitting still, I'm so excited about seeing her surprise. I tiptoe over to the corner where the baby is asleep and almost give a little kiss on her cheek. When Sadaf finally turns, I pull out the phone and thrust it toward her. My grin feels like it's out of control.

"What is this?" she says, wiping her hands on the ends of her dupatta. "It's a phone, silly," I say. "For you. You keep it." I wave it at her and she slowly takes it.

"What did you get me a phone for?" she asks, turning it over in her hands, pressing a button.

"You need to charge it first," I explain quickly before she lets the excitement slip away. Then she looks up at me, asks me how much I had to pay for it, and her voice is sad and her mouth is a straight line. I tell her it wasn't expensive at all, I got a good deal, and it's a gift so that's all I'm going to say, and it's a useful gift because now she can call anyone she wants to. She looks at me and a lot of seconds go by—sneaking out with the last pieces of temporary joy—and she tells me in a flat voice that she will start spending money on calling when we can spare it. I watch her put the phone inside a box that she keeps locked and I think, *That's not a safe place*, but I don't say it.

I haven't been to see Chacha for some time and that is remiss of me. I owe him an update. The heat after the rains is worse than before and I am sweating by the time I reach the street where his shop is. The carpet of plastic bags is dry, but the smell and the flies have been spurred on by the rising temperatures to go higher and spread wider. I hold my breath and hurry to the door, gasping for air once I reach inside. Chacha greets me serenely from behind the counter. I wonder if he takes the smell home in his beard every night. I see that I'm not the only one there today. Chacha's other nephew, Jawed, is there as well. He's been looking for work for longer than I have. We talk about this and that, the three of us, but part of me is imagining being in the bus, in my uniform—I hope there's a uniform—where there are no bad smells and flies, only the vibration of the engine and the steering wheel and driving, driving, driving with the wind from the air conditioner on my face. Chacha asks us to stay and have a cup of tea with him.

When I say no, he looks at me and then says tactfully that he'll add it to our accounts because we're old friends. The shop is warm and the chai is warm and the talk is slow. He offers us biscuits and when we refuse he looks at us in an avuncular fashion and puts small packets of Gluco next to each of our cups, adding them to his account book in his neat, small letters.

I am surprised when, a few days later, Sadaf asks me about the bulletproof bus. I tell her about all the phone calls, and she asks me why I haven't called the Cheema person yet and I don't have an answer for that. She clucks her tongue impatiently and tells me that she's going to sell the phone I bought her so that she can buy her baby a pair of shoes. I want to remind her that the baby doesn't walk yet but—wisely—I keep my mouth shut.

Sadaf tells me the next evening that she is going to start work at a lady's house.

Sweeping, washing clothes, maybe a little cooking. Anguish grips my heart.

"You'll be her maasi," I say.

"I don't care," says Sadaf. "I should have done this sooner." Her tone is lighter than I've heard it in the whole year we've been married. It amazes me that she really doesn't mind pushing a wet cloth over someone else's marble floor and wringing other people's dirty clothes with her hands. She hums as she cooks dinner—peas, potatoes, and two rotis—and tickles the baby. I eat my food in silence, leaving half of my roti in case the baby gets hungry later. I hope Sadaf notices.

When I was younger, I was told every day by my parents that I had to take care of my older brother. He was irresponsible and I had to be a good example to him. But when I wasn't looking, he slipped away and never came back. My father died from worry one year later and my mother died six months after that. I told myself I would never let myself get talked into taking care of a difficult situation again, and then when I turned twenty-five, I ended up marrying Sadaf, who had been married once before to a bad man. Not only was she divorced, she had a small girl, a baby. I couldn't convince my aunt and uncle that she was a good woman. They don't speak to me anymore.

The next day, I watch her and the baby leave right after breakfast. Then I take out my phone and my scrap of paper with its collection of phone numbers.

What I get from calling Mr. Cheema is another name and number, and I call this one—a Mr. Anwar—right away. By this time, I have zero nervousness. Mr. Anwar speaks fast, his words slanting upward like questions. He says that I must have ten years of driving experience, a valid license, four copies of passport-sized photographs of myself, and a letter of recommendation from my last or current place of employment. I must also be able to speak English. All this he tells me in less than a minute, and after he says "Khuda hafiz" and the call disconnects, I try to hold on to what he has told me. Pictures, letter, license, experience. And English.

I'll have to wait for Sadaf to get paid so that I can get a picture taken at a Kodak studio. I'm sure the juice seller won't write a letter for me but my friend Abid might. We were in school together until class five, after which both of us left to get work at a mechanic's. He has his own mechanic shop now—well, he and his brother-in-law. He'll write me a letter, I'm sure.

And I know my English. There is nobody home, but I still look around before saying in a low voice, "Hello, my name is Asif." My face feels warm and my armpits are instantly damp and I think, *I can't let myself look like this after just one sentence.* I try again, though it is hard to make my tongue glide smoothly from sound to sound. I feel better after the tenth time and I then say, "How are you?" and "Welcome to Karachi." It is only ten in the morning and a good time to go see Abid.

My scalp itches in the humidity and I walk slowly so that I don't sweat too much. I see Jawed standing by the chai cart and he lazily raises a hand in greeting. I nod a salaam and look away as if preoccupied purposefully, but he falls into step beside me.

"I heard you got a job," he says. His voice is lazy, too. His statement feels like a trick question.

"Not yet," I say cautiously. "Have you?"

"Now who's going to hire a good-for-nothing like me?" He grins and I relax.

"Come to Chacha's shop for lunch," he says, and I tell him I'll be there.

Abid's letter of recommendation is in English and I am reading it slowly, silently, because Sadaf and the baby are asleep. There are five lines, and when I reach the end I feel good.

He has been generous, calling me a hard worker and a good employee. He told me he's writing this lie of a letter only because I have a wife and a baby to take care of, and I need the job. I don't mind him saying that because he is an old friend.

I let myself think about the bus. From the outside, it looks like any other bus, every inch of it covered in patterns in different colors. There's a line of poetry on the back framed by two peacocks sticking out their chests as if they wrote it. There are two eyes on the front outlined in paint-kohl, with the headlights as pupils. Underneath the paint, the body of the bus is made to protect the bodies of the passengers. The doors of the bus must remain closed for the duration of the tour. They pay a lot of money for that kind of protection so they can safely take their cameras and wallets to the parts of the city where people like us live. People who look thin with desperation and want to mug or kill better-dressed people. At least, that's what those others think. When I drive that bus, I'll be enclosed in the same safe zone as those people. Even the windshield and windows are bulletproof.

It shouldn't be long now before Sadaf gets her first pay. I don't think she will mind if I use some of it for the photographs that I need to give with my job application.

Then one evening I see Jawed at the chai cart again. His

scruffy beard is gone and his hair looks combed. He saunters toward me, grinning.

"Asif! Salaam," he calls out.

For some reason, the return greeting sticks in my throat.

"Remind me to buy you some mithai with my first pay," he says. "I got a job."

"Really? Where?" I manage to ask.

"You know that new bus they've got running through the city? Karachi King Express. I'm going to be its new driver." Jawed's grin is genuine and wide. One of his teeth is slightly crooked and there is a mole under his left earlobe. And still he talks. "I owe a lot to Chacha Fazal, I do. He gave me the idea and all the encouragement. He never gave up on me." Jawed's voice gets thick with emotion.

I don't remember what I say to him—congratulations, probably—before I walk away in a hurry, away from his grin and the picture of him in the smooth driver's seat of the bulletproof bus.

I walk fast and I know where I am going. The plastic bags look a uniform bluish brown in the twilight, almost like a road. They don't smell so bad anymore or maybe I've become used to their stink. I probably come here too often. Through the door, I see Chacha behind the counter, his beard blowing in the air from a small fan he's got standing on the glass. A gift from his nephew, probably. I push down on the door handle, but he has locked the door. I hit it with my fist, and again, and again, but nothing happens. He looks at me once, then picks up his phone.

I realize I don't know what he's capable of doing, so I turn around for home.

I hold up my hands, and in the dark I try to show Sadaf the

difference between the right one and the left one. The thumb of the left hand is swollen, and there are cuts on the right one but they don't hurt. I tell this to her in a whisper so that she doesn't wake up. She is less angry with me when she's sleeping.

TOURISM

A HIDDEN GEM

WELCOME TO GILGIT-BALTISTAN, FORMERLY known as the Northern Areas of Pakistan. The gorgeous scenery promises to stun all visitors. (Please note that it does not promise to restore you, just as the sea by your city in the south never did. Restoration is solely your own responsibility, and the mountains, rivers, and fresh air cannot be held accountable if you fail to heal.) Before going farther north, you must make a stopover in the city of Gilgit. We recommend that you spend no more than one day and one night there. Other travelers say that a small waterfall nearby is a must-see, and it is true that it is lovely, but you are tired. You must give yourself some time to get used to the altitude, to acclimatize to your escape, to ease into your freedom. Take a Xanax and go to sleep.

It is easy to hire a car and a driver to visit the Hunza Valley. Rates can be negotiated—four to six thousand rupees. On the way up, you can spend some of your vacation budget on a local rug, a local hat, a local vase, or a local ashtray (unless you quit cigarettes because your children started to look small and sad through the curling smoke). You can buy several packets of local dried apricots, so your children can transform from the pale, thin ghosts of a broken home to the rosy-cheeked children of this region. It is poor penance for the choices you have made, but it's a start. Their mother would be pleased by the inoffensive, neutral nature of the gift. You do not need to buy her anything; you have no relation with her now—other than the fact that she has lived with your children in another house for two years. You might not know this, but that day you locked yourself in your car and turned off the air-conditioning so you could sweat yourself to death—and she, dry-eyed and nonwhimsical, broke the back window with a rock so you could breathe—was the day she decided she did not want to know you anymore.

The Karakoram Highway goes through the Karakoram Range. See the snow-covered mountains sloping down to green valleys and the rivers winding through farms and orchards? The result is unbelievably picturesque. The road conditions are excellent and the driver is experienced, so feel free to fall asleep in the back seat without fear of plunging over the highway's edge.

THE HUNZA VALLEY AND THE SURROUNDING MOUNTAINS

It is best to arrive in daylight to take in the full splendor of the area. Observe the stunning mountains that ring the verdant Hunza Valley: Rakaposhi (seven thousand, seven hundred, and eighty-eight meters above sea level), Ultar Sar (seven thousand, three hundred, and eighty-eight meters above sea level), Bubli-mating (six thousand meters above sea level), and many others. Tear the thin plastic wrapper off your notebook. Unscrew the cap of your shiny new pen to write down these numbers. Write down, as well, that Rakaposhi is the twenty-seventh highest mountain in the world. Note that you are puny, crushable, cowardly. (If you insist upon factual accuracy, add a postscript to your entry: that it was because you cried so easily, in your cubicle and in your bed, that your coworkers shuffled away in awkward silence and your wife left.)

The first sight of these wonders will make you shiver. You will imagine that the cool air entering your lungs has come from puffs of fresh snow falling on those high mountaintops. You will want to drink water from a glacier. You will want to rub snowmelt into your face in a circular motion until all the pores in your skin wake up, then numb, then deaden.

You must get up early to see how the rising sun spreads like melting butter on the snowcapped peaks. It is a glorious sight. When you see farmers already hard at work in the valley, backs bent over rows of furrowed earth, you will feel momentarily ashamed of the sleep you are still rubbing from your eyes. Not everybody here farms, of course. There is a woman somewhere (light-skinned, light-eyed, dark-haired) who wakes early and lies in bed wondering if she should get up today. (You will pass by her later, after you've had your breakfast in the hotel dining room.)

The butter, jams, and preserves made by the people of Hunza must be tried. The health benefits of the local diet have been known for centuries. Taste the fiti bread with apricot oil. The flavor will transport you away from memories—away from the confines of your dining table (back at your Karachi home), which your wife placed under the heavy chandelier she bought for herself as a reward for being married to you. Try a refreshing drink called chamus, also made from apricots. Its tartness will dull the memory of the grotesque parody that was your family life, of the unblinking eyes your wife and children turned toward you, their mouths like black holes, needing, demanding, devouring. They did not know they were talking down a dry well.

After breakfast, go for a walk among the poplars and the firs of the hotel grounds. Their scent is better than that of the grass at your home—which you pulled out in handfuls one morning while your children watched and their mother shook her head and tapped her watch. (You went to work that day with grass stains on your pants, and the trash bag covering the broken rear window blew loose on the drive.)

You can also take a brisk walk down to the farms and watch people till the soil, sow seeds, and do other things you think farmers must do all the time. Cows and woolly sheep dot the landscape, grazing the green grass. Their moos and baas appropriately fill the auditory component of the setting. The people there do not speak loudly because they know that voices carry from one end of the valley to the other. This makes them very private, which is also the reason they do not initiate a conversation with you. (It is not because they think badly of you.) Feel free to pick an apple or two from the trees around you. Nobody will ask you, *Why* or *How dare you*. Taste the sweetness of the fruit and roll your sleeve back to let the juice dribble down your arm. The farms are also a great place from which to photograph the surrounding peaks. On a clear day, you can easily capture all of them, the landscape's contrasts coming out beautifully: emerald grass, golden crop, white snow, blue sky, purple flowers, black-and-white cow, and browned, bent farmer. If, in the course of your morning wandering, your brain begins to detect pain, click the shutter faster.

As you walk back up to your hotel, you will pass old people sitting on low walls in front of their homes, their mouths caved in from toothlessness. You might think that if you stop and smile, an aged woman will pat the ancient, sun-warmed stone next to her, inviting you to sit down and put your weary head on her lap while she brushes the hair off your forehead like a mother. You might imagine that her lap will smell of bread and simple white flowers. You might want to stay there until your bones and her bones fuse and petrify, because in stillness is forgetting is peace.

Do not attempt to do so. The older population here speaks only Burushaski and will not understand you. Someone younger than fifty—perhaps a waiter at your hotel—will understand you better in a language in which you are already fluent (Urdu or English), so do not strain your own learning abilities. You are, after all, here to get healed.

HISTORY OF THE PEOPLE

Some say that the Hunzakuts are descendants of the army of Alexander the Great. DNA tests—carried out with enthusiasm—have proven this claim to be false. The people here do not show signs of disappointment. They go on peacefully culti-vating their land. What's more, their language has little or no genealogical relationship with any other language in the world. It stands isolated. (Like you, in your room in your hotel slippers and hotel bathrobe, making garbled alien sounds, saying, over and over again, "Sorry.")

HISTORY OF THE MOUNTAINS

The Karakoram Range is the result of orogeny and subduction: long ago, before the beginning of your own metamorphosis—before you broke the mirror your wife had insisted on fixing above the dresser because you did not understand who it was you were looking at anymore—the edge of the Indian continental plate was pushed under by the Asian continental plate. You may want to write that down, too.

HISTORY OF THE WOMAN YOU PASSED BY IN THE AFTERNOON

She is thirty years old and watches the people who arrive with the different seasons. She has watched you walk on the road with belabored steps—the incline in places is quite steep. She makes and sells fruit preserves to hotels and shops. You have eaten her apple preserve at your breakfast table. She also takes her two sheep grazing but prefers the smell of the fruit to that of the animals. She cares for an old aunt in whose house she lives. The day she first saw you, she tucked pieces of orange rind in her hair before going to sleep, to kill the smell of the sheep.

HISTORY OF YOU

When you were born, you had thick black hair on your head and a nurse gasped, worrying your poor mother. Your father was patted on his back in congratulations of his achievement. When you went to school, you had a crush on your geology teacher, which is why you still collect rock samples. When you were seventeen, you wanted to live five more lives so you could spend one life each studying history, linguistics, anthropology, literature, and astronomy. When your father found you writing poetry, he ripped your notebook down the spine and across the pages and swept your table clean. He said that you might as well have been born dead, the way you were turning out. You graduated with a degree in business and got married to a lovely, suitable girl; you lived in a pretty house with a pretty garden (it even had a small pond because your wife said the children needed it), the whole of it paid for in easy installments; you went to work and came home and you went to work and came home; and then one day (you've come to collapse the years into days, almost all the days indistinguishable, intolerable) you drove into a tree and cut your forehead on the windshield.

THINGS TO DO

On a fine morning, you can walk up to the forts whose rhyming names tickle visitors: Baltit and Altit. They have formal rooms—where rulers met sycophants—as well as prisoners' cells into which men—and maybe women—were thrown. Listen to the guide tell the histories of such places. The mention of war will make you tighten your jaw and shake your head. You do not like violence.

Touch the ancient walls and lie down with your face on the cool stone floor. Do you hear hooves? The strike of a spoon in a metal pot? The scratch of a quill on paper as someone writes a secret verse? Write down all the details, the unusual facts, and the clichés. The forts are open from 8:00 a.m. until 6:00 p.m.

Among the many lakes in the region is Attabad Lake, almost thirty kilometers from Hunza Valley. It is the result of a landslide that blocked the Hunza River; the new lake displaced thousands of people from twenty-one villages. Do not feel bad about admiring the water despite its murderous beginnings, but also, look ashamed that some people have it worse than you. Take a ride in one of the narrow, colorful boats denting the shores of the lake. Locals use them to go from one side to the other; they ride together with their animals and clothes and food. You can choose to hire your own boat if you would rather not have too many feelings crowding one little vessel. Once aboard, turn your attention to the beautiful ripples forming around your boat as you cross. In your notebook, call the water *turquoise* or *teal*, not *blue*. You can also make notes about the locals in those other little vessels, how the gentle rocking of their boats seems to have lulled them into hypnotized silence or perhaps into remembrance of their homes under the water. Ask your guide about the cause of the color of the lake. "Are there tiles at the bottom? Special, teal-colored fish swimming about in there?" He will laugh (probably) and tell you that the only interesting things at the bottom of the lake are the people swelling on their beds. That and the still-alive trees, the frightened leaves peering through the water. (It is recommended that you leave him a generous tip at the end of your cruise.)

As you return to your hotel, write down all the pretty names you have heard so far: Hunza (the river that got choked by the rocks, turning it into a hundred-meter-deep lake), Gojal (the valley that flooded), and Tupopdan (the peak that looked down upon it all). Gulmit, Shishkat, and Ghulkin (the downriver villages that drowned from the water spilling over the dam; the lake lowered, but still remained). You might want to talk about them with the girl who sleeps with orange rinds in her hair.

OFF THE BEATEN TRACK

Borith Lake is a peaceful, small body of water. Your hired driver will be happy to take you there for an extra two hundred rupees. Off the Karakoram Highway, your car will ascend a one-and-three-quarters-meter-wide unpaved path covered with rocks with no guardrail between you and a two-thousand- meter drop. The possibility of dying will push you into your seat and your legs will sweat while your mouth dries out. In no particular order, you will see images of your children, your desk when you were ten, your coffee mug in the office kitchen (World's Best Manager). Whimpering now, you will wonder if the car will flip over, midair, during its free fall. The driver will turn to look at you and grin, the hairs in his mustache spreading out like an accordion. "Why do you worry?" he will say and laugh loudly. "We all have to die one day. I am an expert at driving here." The return to level ground will fill you with exhilaration, and you will uncurl and try to joke with the driver. He will smile obligingly. Ask him to stop the car at the orange-rind woman's shop. It is an unassuming little structure on the side of the road with the name Roshan Bano Crafts on top. Roshan Bano is not the woman's name, but she is inside, waiting. Buy whatever you can because you are alive.

WORKS OF A LASTING IMPRESSION

There is poverty here, but it is a genteel kind, hidden behind layers of good manners and hard work. You will not find many—or any—people complaining, but take a good look around. The schools are tiny, the clothes are patched, the closest big hospital is two hours away. The more you realize the facts behind the smiles, the more you thrill at the prospect of making a difference, of doing something meaningful, of leaving a legacy, however small. Removing that twig from the path as you walk toward the school near your hotel is a good start. Peek in one of the two windows and see the rows of eager students sitting at desks with chipped corners. See them share books that have been passed down for the last five years, ink stained and a little torn. There are so many ways to convince yourself of your goodness—to thoroughly overwrite the reason for your existence—that you would have to reintroduce yourself to the reflection you smashed. "The doer of *good*." "The *helper*." "The beacon of *light*." It is recommended that you pursue social work only after you're sure you'll stick with it, and you are far away from that firmness of mind. Step away from the window before the children see you. Nobody likes a quitter, not even the smiling, gentle locals.

WHAT TO DO ON DAYS YOU CANNOT GET OUT OF BED

Turn on the TV and watch old movies. Find a local channel and learn the language. If, by late afternoon, you feel able to throw off your blanket, shuffle to the window and pull apart the curtains. Watch night descend into the bowl of the valley and then upon the sides of the mountains. Watch lights turn on in houses far below. Watch the stars come out in breathtaking clarity. What do they remind you of? Look again at the light-years of night speeding toward you, and hastily draw the curtains before running back to bed. Take out your notebook and read it, committing all facts and observations to memory. Write what you remember about the woman in the shop, if she smelled like oranges, if your soul contracted or expanded in her presence. As your eyelids get heavy, wonder again about the teal of that lake, if there are rocks in its bed worth collecting.

WHEN TO GO

All four seasons exhibit gloriousness, so consider traveling here the whole year round. If you visit in summer you can choose from mulberries, peaches, and apples. Autumn promises vivid red and yellow leaves. In winter, you can watch snowfall and darkness from your cozy hotel window. On difficult nights, you can eat dried apricots and wait for gray morning light. Remember to wear a woolen hat.

We must say that spring is the best season in which to visit. The slopes of the mountains change color continually, providing many moments of wonder. You can stare at them all day, afraid of what they may say. Sometimes they speak in winds that push down—right into your face—confusing echoes: *Who do you think you are?* and *Who are you now?*

SUGGESTIONS FOR THE TRAVELER

The Hunzakuts are a simple, loving people, and legend has it that they live extraordinarily long lives. Most are educated. The orange-rind woman likes reading books on history. If you ask her to go for a walk with you, she will agree, and then stop by her home to tell her aunt that she will be right back. Walk with her as far up the slopes as possible. Wear the hat you bought from her shop. Do not mistake her quietness for shyness. She will gladly tell you all that she knows: that the glaciers are slowly shrinking, that sometimes she thinks the mountains look shorter but then she blinks and they are as they've always been.

She will not get out of breath—she has climbed these heights all her life—and will wait patiently for your lungs to get used to their new capacity. Like a mountain goat, she will run up steep, rocky hills to pick you hard-to-reach wildflowers as you watch with your heart in your throat, worried about her safety. In the winter, she will cook soup for you and collect firewood. If you tell her that you want to go swimming in the teal lake, she will not say no.

The Hunzakuts have a strong moral compass. Always return to your separate places after your excursions. Negotiate with your hotel for a year's room rental.

TRAVEL TIPS

In the summer, cut your hair close to the scalp, and in the winter, let it grow. Do not call what used to be home; do not look back. Buy additional notebooks and pens; you are going to come to know more and more still. When you finally decide to explore the teal lake properly, consider walking there from the hotel. Eat a piece of dried apricot every five hundred meters; it will help with any dizziness you might experience. If fear creeps up and covers your heart, run. Do not stop until your chest begins to hurt. Dress in layers. The sun can be quite strong here—sunblock is recommended. When you reach the lake, take off your shoes and your watch. Leave the woman with the orange rinds at the shore to guard your belongings and slowly walk into the water. The cold water and the sight of the mountains in front of you will cover your skin in gooseflesh and make your eyes sting. Your heart will beat faster, but that could be the altitude. Keep walking, feeling with your feet the color of the rocks, picking up the blue ones. When you run out of space in your pockets, start tucking the rocks into the waist of your jeans. You will want to keep walking until the bed of the lake falls away and the heaviness in the cuffs of your pants matches that in your waistband. Swim a little farther and sink a little more, then put your head under the water. Stones, algae, ice, wood, glass, clocks, fossils of faces—puzzled and mocking—are all lit up under expensive, hand-painted lamps. There is movement, you realize. Raise your head out of the water and see the woman gliding toward you. Notice the wind grazing lightly against her eyes and how her pupils don't waver as her strong arms make circular motions. You are at once surprised and moved by the grip of her muscles around your waist. As she takes out the rocks, she tells you their names before letting them fall back to their depths.

BEAUTIFUL

AT THE ORPHANAGE, ISMAT liked to tell us lies about our origins. I knew mine by heart.

With pride in her voice that made me grind my teeth, she would say, "Your mother brought you here when you were just eight days old."

"She did not even have a name for me," I would counter.

"She said you were a gift she couldn't keep."

"She knew she could dump me here like a bag of old shoes; she knew someone would pick it up."

"She was so shy—wouldn't show her face. Slept outside on the pavement for a week, refusing to go, her mouth covered."

When I was six, I began to wet my bed in the night. One such time a nurse, eyes swollen with broken sleep, pushed me into the bathroom and without preamble stripped off my soiled clothes and poured cold water over me from a bucket.

Drying me off, she muttered, "Haraam zaadi." Bastard. I thought it was an interesting word; I had heard it in a movie.

When I became a little older and understood all of its implications, I still didn't mind it. And by the time I was no longer a child, I agreed with it on some level. Who knew what my parents were? Tainted or wholesome, together or apart. Alive or dead. They could be anyone, anywhere. It did not matter to me.

Ismat tried hard to keep our lives steady and uneventful, but sometimes the whims of donors took us in unexpected directions. Around the time I was eight, someone sent the orphanage cans of yellow paint and right away Ismat hired a man to redo our TV room walls, to make them more cheerful. But what had seemed like an overabundance to us turned out to be just enough for a portion of the walls. So we watched our programs surrounded by walls in alternating states. All this I considered normal, how everyone lived.

I must have loved Ismat when I was a child, but later she became nothing more than the woman who ran the orphanage, a shape in the background.

When I was fourteen or fifteen the girls I knew graduated from watching variety shows on TV at five in the afternoon to watching drama serials at eight every night. They wished they had the nice homes and the beautiful mothers and the shopping excursions. It seemed to me they had entered a new phase where they enjoyed being sad. Even the way they sat was an attitude of meek defeat, on the floor with their chins on their knees, arms wrapped around their legs. The nurses sighed right along with them, reveling in their morose moments. One of the girls would say, "Who will marry us?" and—with saccharine tenderness—the nurses would say, "You will have a family of your own one day." But they didn't really care; I could tell. And the sad girls never noticed the smirks on their faces, which is why I felt they deserved the insincerity. That, and because I thought they were beautiful. To me, they seemed to have all grown into one graceful body.

The girls who didn't find homes tried their luck with marriages Ismat arranged for them; those who couldn't get married had by then stayed at the orphanage for so long they eventually exchanged their beds in the girls' rooms for beds in the nurses' rooms. The men Ismat found for the girls to marry did not look like ones we saw on TV but they had respectable professions: shopkeepers, salesmen, tailors. Something in the way these men sat and half-smiled showed that they knew the ways of the world. The girls never said no to these proposals, and I could understand why. There was something exciting about the whole arrangement. Men loomed over us, took up more space than us. They seemed hard to please, but we imagined that we could belong to them forever.

The first time I saw Babar the rat catcher was when he was getting out of the driver's side of a small van with a cartoon of worried rats painted on the side. He was well-dressed: black pants with sharp creases and a short-sleeved blue shirt. He carried a large bag that looked very heavy. It was probably full of rat poison. The proximity of a man to so much danger thrilled me.

I found him in the corridor just inside the door; a nurse said in a bored voice, "How long will this take?" The rat catcher answered, "Could be an hour, ma'am." They both saw me then; the man gave me a smile. His hair and his eyes were black-brown; he looked even better up close.

Bending his head a little deferentially, he said to the nurse, "Perhaps this young lady could show me around. Would save you trouble."

She chewed the inside of her cheek for a moment, then said, "Yes, why not," and left us alone.

We went all around the orphanage together. Sometimes he went down on his hands and knees, checking corners, his torch in his mouth, making ticks and notes on his clipboard. His voice floated up from the floor: "There is evidence of rats." He tucked away little black trays filled with something thick and gray. "Trapping glue," he said. The moment I felt time stand still was when we were in the storeroom with the carton full of faded green curtains. With gloved hands, Babar gently turned over a fold of green, revealing tiny, black ovals dotting the material. We stared at the evidence, him in satisfaction and me in thrall of his capability. If he had told me to go ahead and touch the dots to see how they crumbled I would have. He took out boxes with red skulls and crossbones on the lids. "Dangerous, powerful bait inside," he said. "The rats eat this once, then go back to their nests and die." He put down the last box. "I've never been inside an orphanage before, you know. Always thought it would be a little like a hospital." He gave a short laugh. "Certainly didn't expect it to have someone as pretty as you." He stood looking at me for one second, three seconds.

I held my breath and wondered what was going to happen next.

"Well." He clicked his pen shut. "I'll be back for another check, same time." He held out his clipboard, looking slightly embarrassed. "Here. Take this. I would have liked to give you something special for all your help, but this is all I have at the moment."

I put the clipboard under my pillow that night and fell asleep thinking warm thoughts about his knowledge, his restraint.

I had long been consumed with the need to link myself to a man and his love. The first one I had tried to get to like me was Ismat's driver; I brought him cups of tea, pretending to be shy, and he took them with a smile, his small mustache like a centipede. Very soon he invited me to sit next to him on the bench under the tree, his radio playing somewhere by his feet. Every time I sat there he put his hand on my knee and my body tingled and I thought, *This is what love must feel like.* But one day he wasn't there. I found out that Ismat had fired him; I did not speak to her for a month.

Then there was the sweeper who came by every week or so. He squatted over the floor and swept away soil, leaves, water. When I told him his hard work must exhaust him, he said he was pleased someone appreciated it. Moving a broom over and over again was hard work, but it did give him strong muscles, he said. He let me feel them and stroked my hair and said I was a clever girl. Again, I felt that joyful surge of love. We had met just two times when he stopped coming over. My misery brought on a fever; Ismat sat by my bed, laying strips of cold, damp cloth on my forehead. She murmured things I didn't understand. For a short while, at the height of my fever—104, I was told later—I accepted the roles Ismat played in my life. Mother, payer, keeper. She spent nights on a mattress on the floor next to me.

As I got better, the sight of her began to remind me of the sweeper and what I didn't have anymore. Her presence became unbearable; one afternoon I took the medicine bottle from her hand and broke it on the floor.

With Babar, it was different. I wasn't going to let him leave me surprised with sadness. I watched every day from eleven until noon for his van, and when he came by, I greeted him and let my pleasure show on my face even though Ismat was right there or maybe because she was right there. I said, "I will help with the rat check. The nurses are not good at this." Ismat hesitated a moment, then said thank you, and later, as I trailed Babar, holding his bag, I imagined her sitting at her old, scratched desk, shoulders and breasts sagging in defeat because she hadn't been able to keep everyone away from me.

Standing by a tray with a dead rat in it, Babar gave me a present, a hairbrush with a glittery handle. As I moved my fingers over the smooth plastic to show him my admiration of it, he closed his hand around my wrist and held it up. "Look at you. So weak. They don't feed you well here. And your clothes, they don't even fit you."

Babar let go of my hand.

"What does your name mean?" I felt audacious, older, unlike myself.

He smiled. "Lion. Big and strong and protecting. And yours? What does Khajista mean?"

"I don't know."

"Khajista. Your name is dry as a biscuit."

"Ismat chose it for me."

"How old are you?"

"I'm nineteen."

"Khajista." He tilted his head to one side and narrowed his eyes. Then, rapidly, "Khajista, bring me tea. Khajista, find me my socks. Khajista, let's have a picnic by the sea, have ice cream, watch a movie."

Breathlessly, I said, "OK."

I didn't tell anyone about him; I was not friends with the girls there. There was very little that they and I understood about one another. They liked to braid each other's hair and pick names for their future children. I had once furtively tried to practice on my own hair so I could show them my skills; though I tugged angrily at the snarls with my fingers, eyes smarting from the pull on my scalp, I did not look like them. I liked to sneak into the kitchen to steal milk powder and eat it in fistfuls until I doubled over from stomach pain. The girls practiced cooking. I plucked hair from my arms with my fingers. Sometimes the nurses caught me in one of these acts. Then they clicked their tongues and said it was because I had never seen my mother or my father that I behaved so strangely. They believed that was the reason for any kind of trouble a girl here could be having— poor digestion or teeth that stick out or a painful period.

I stopped doing those things after I met Babar. It was as if someone had given my brain a strong painkiller. I found things to give to him, a notebook, a pen. I planned things to say to him so he would think I was bright and interesting. I looked through my meager collection of clothes for something to wear for his next visit and found nothing that matched or was not worn out. I stole a shirt I liked from another girl's drawer, but it would not go down past my chest. At night I pictured his eyebrows; they were like wings. I tried to sleep a lot because sleep made the time go by faster. I had dreams. In one, I was holding his bag of poison; in another, I was letting Ismat comb my hair, the teeth getting caught in my frizzy tangles before breaking through. Sometimes I practiced how I would introduce Babar to the nurses and the girls, imagined surprise and jealousy spreading like lightning over their faces.

Ismat had only ever been able to get me one suitor, a man in his fifties. A shopkeeper with a sixteen-year-old son who stayed most of the time with his ex-wife—so he wouldn't be any trouble. Ismat said, "This might be your only chance, Khajista." The day the man and his mother came over, I sat in the drawing room with knots in my stomach, keeping my eyes lowered, just as I had been told. I glanced at the man; he was a mountain. The mother said a few brief sentences to Ismat and nothing to me at all. Five minutes later, they left. A few days later, a nurse told me that the woman had called Ismat and said no; I seemed too large and dull to make her son a good wife.

I locked myself into a bathroom and examined my body. My legs and waist were thick, my face was square. There was extra flesh on my stomach which I held with my hands and tried to squeeze flat. I had the kind of form that could make people angry, that was harder to forgive. I wondered if I had always looked like this; I had never seen any photographs of myself from when I was younger—there weren't any. After my self-examination, I returned to the TV room and pulled more hair.

Babar had told me he would visit again in exactly ten days. I got dressed up for him this time. I covered my face with light-colored pressed powder I'd found in a nurse's bag. I even tried to put on a red-brown lipstick. In one of the rooms, I gave him his presents and he said they were just what he needed and put them inside his bag.

He started checking the traps, but they were empty. He was disappointed and pretended to be upset with me. "You have distracted me from being a good rat catcher," he growled, then laughed. But I had something to show him and I could hardly wait. Finally, in the last room we came to it: two rats stuck in a tray of glue. "Look," I said, pointing at my present to him. "I found them two days ago." The rats were facing the same way, their claws and eyes completely still, fur lying close to their bodies. I watched Babar.

"I've never seen two in a trap before," he said, his voice low and full of reverence. He squatted on the floor and used the end of a pen to part their fur. "Boy and a girl."

I had not known that. "They were together till the end."

Babar laughed. "They could be brother and sister, you know." In one quick motion he dropped the tray into the bag and stood up. "Did you know rat bite sickness can make holes in the heart? The brain, too."

I waited nervously for him to tell me when we could see each other again. He peeled off his gloves.

"I need your help with something. Will you do it, Khajista? Will you help me?"

I nodded hard. He beckoned me to come with him. Quickly we walked toward the main door and stopped outside Ismat's office. The door was ajar; there was nobody inside. Babar went over to her desk, his shoes making no sound over the worn carpet. He took a bent paperclip out of his pocket and stuck one end of it into a drawer. In another second he slid it open. I did not understand what he was doing, but I was afraid if I questioned him, he would tell me to go. When he whispered to me, I jumped. "There's money in there," he said. "Take it out." Set on top of papers was a fat pile of currency, stapled in the corner, fresh from a bank. Here was fear again; if I let myself think about Ismat—her voice, her old slippers, the bottle of nail polish she kept thinning with water to make it last longer even though the pink was now too pale—I would lose this moment forever.

Babar said, "You won't get caught. Get the money. It's probably for you anyway."

If this was a test of love, I wanted to do well. I closed my hands around the money, took it out, and pushed the drawer shut.

"Good, brave girl," Babar whispered, his face flushed. He held open his bag in front of me and I dropped the money into it.

Quickly now, he walked outside to his van and I followed him, suddenly feeling dull and lifeless. This was it; he was going away for good now. I was of no use to him anymore, and I had never been of use to anyone here either. He unlocked the door and tossed the bag in, so casually.

"Well. You are quite the champion."

"Yes," I said, my voice wobbling.

He took out his keys and stood turning them over in his hands. Finally he looked up, his face red. "I am a good person, Khajista. How would you like to come away with me?"

"With you?" The dullness began to recede; again, my heart beat faster.

"You can do much better than staying here." He sounded surer with each word. Then he grabbed my hands. "She hasn't even given you her last name, yet she calls you her daughter." He was mistaken; Ismat had never called me her daughter.

"This money can be ours, Khajista," he said. "And even more rightfully yours. You deserve it. Will you come with me?"

I told him yes.

That same evening I ran away from the orphanage, hiding in Babar's van. All I had with me were the old shoes on my feet and the clothes I wore. As we drove away, him laughing and slapping his thigh at pulling off this stunt, I thought, *This is just like a scene from a movie.* For a while, I wished I'd been able to bring with me some things I'd had my eyes on at the orphanage, a beaded bag, a chiffon dupatta. But then Babar stopped next to a man selling ice cream and bought me two scoops, and I forgot about old things.

I don't remember all the girls at the orphanage, but some I still recall very well, especially the ones who were nearer my age.

I remember Ismat of course, but I have been careful in choosing which moments and exchanges to retain. The voice of hers that I carry in my head is from when I was sick. And once, when I was very young, I smiled back at her; I must have.

I remember Ismat of course, but I have been careful in choosing which moments and exchanges to retain. The voice of hers that I carry in my head is from when I was sick. And once, when I was very young, I smiled back at her; I must have.

She would be happy to know I am doing well, I'm sure of that. With her money, Babar and I were able to start a good life. Now in the daytime, he sees to his rat-catching business, buying new traps and advanced poisons, reciting to me excitedly the list of chemicals and their percentages of success. In the evening, he plays with our children, who wear new clothes several times a year. We have a nice little flat across from a school. Lately I have been going to my balcony when the school day ends. Licking the dust covering the ledge off my fingers, I scan the faces of the little girls as they stand on the pavement before getting into cars and vans. An absurd hope bubbles up in me; maybe if I follow one of those girls all the way to her home, I'll discover that she is the daughter of a girl I had known. And maybe she, older and friendly now, would invite me in, and we would talk about Ismat and how we used to be and how beautiful we all are now in our completeness.

FOREIGNERS

PLEASE HAVE TWO SEATS since there are two of you. Now we are nicely arranged. I'm sorry we have to be divided like this: me on this side of the plastic partition and you on the other. This is supposed to protect me from harm, even though they took away your bags and ran scanners down your persons the moment you were allowed to enter the unremarkable premises of the American Consulate. Admit it—it's better in here than the disorderly mess of Karachi outside. It makes me miss the green, dust-free land of my birth: Riverdale, U.S.A.

I hope you didn't take that personally. Kindly put your passports, bank statements, visa applications, photos, birth certificates, marriage certificate, and proof of home ownership over here.

Husband and wife, I see. Married for—hmm, here's my calculator, forty-three years. That is a long time! How have things been? Any rocky moments? Any scars from words that left wounds? I saw how you pulled the chair out for her, sir.

I saw you hand him his glasses, ma'am. Is this what love can look like in old age? Gallantry, dispensing of medicine, helping with the other's failing faculties? Perhaps we will have that discussion another day.

Sir, would you please write your name down on this piece of paper? Bader. Oh, am I saying it wrong? Budder? Close enough, you say. Now please write it in your native script on the same piece of paper. Thank you. Please take a tissue—see the box there?—to wipe the sweat off your forehead.

Would you also write yours both ways, ma'am? Ameenah. You look pleased that I got it right. Look at the smooth curves and dips in the letters of your own language. Positively poetic. I will keep this paper for my records.

I see you have been to the United States of America once before. Why are you going back? You say it's to see your daughter, whom you love dearly. Why is that? No, not why you love her. That is an unfathomable emotion of magnificent proportions, I'm sure. I wouldn't know because my wife and I cannot have children. What I want to know is, why do you want to travel to see her? Oh, congratulations, another grandchild! You don't have to look embarrassed by your bounties, ma'am, unless you think you got them at my expense. Did you? I thought not. In that case, I'm happy for you and your family. We all have our purposes on earth. Your daughter's is to fill it with humans. Mine is to interview visa applicants.

How long are you planning on staying with her? Three long months, you say. Your eager smile gives away that you cannot wait to cook and clean for her and look after her children. Does she stick out in her odd clothes in her adopted land? Does she make mistakes in her pronunciation? Are her *r*'s smooth and thick like a twelve-dollar kale smoothie? Is her house full of the smell of fried onions? The cook we have here makes our kitchen smell like that sometimes. It reminds me of my mother. Her meals were filling, but not very tasty. Oh, your daughter has assimilated fully, you say. She lives in a house in the suburbs, bakes for block parties, and has coffee with the mothers from her son's preschool. Oh yes, this young lady in the picture you've pushed through the narrow space between us looks nothing like you. Your daughter? She wraps her faith around her head in a different fashion than yours, ma'am. Does that worry you? Has she lost her way? Ah, I see, she doesn't discuss her choices with you. You say she proudly represents her religion in interfaith meetings in her city and helps raise money for churches in need of repair. My mother was not a regular churchgoer. She asked me if there were Christian churches here in Karachi, and I told her that there must be because I remembered reading about them once, and that last Christmas I saw a skinny brown Santa in a mall near our neighborhood.

And what is your daughter's name? Nora. Why, that's a name you'll find in the *Book of Baby Names* in my house. It sits on my wife's bedside table. You must speak closer to the partition, sir. She changed her name from Noreen to Nora? Your wife is frowning, sir, and putting her hand on top of yours to make you stop talking. I'd like to hear from her, if you don't mind. You are upset that she discarded the name her grandmother had chosen for her, ma'am? If it makes you feel better, it matters not a whit what your child calls herself because to the American public she looks nothing like a Nora. Now I'd like you to write down her name here on this piece of paper, both ways. Thank you. I will keep this paper and her photo for my records.

Your forms indicate that you also have a son. And where does he live? You understand that I can, of course, ask you this—or any other question at all—because it's one of the powers given to me. I can also use any tone I like. That is another one of my powers. He has been in London since he was twenty-five? London, U.K., or London, U.S.A.? It is imperative that you are specific about these things. London, England? He left his bank job to write about cars in a magazine? You are pursing your lips, sir. I will note that right here on my legal pad. Perhaps I should enter it into my computer, but there doesn't seem to be a field on the form in which to register your disapproval. Then again, I do prefer the feel of the movement of an expensive nib over heavy grammage paper. Just between you and me, they have the best stationery here. I've never seen anything like it—not in any other place I've worked. What was my last place of employment? Oh, ma'am, you cannot ask me that. Only I get to ask you things about your life, your opinions, your choices, your past, your future, and your food preferences. You understand, it's just the nature of my job. Sir, you need not glare at your wife like that; she hasn't done anything to jeopardize your chances for visa approval. She only asked out of maternal curiosity, something my own dear mother possessed a lot of until she passed away last year. I got the news over the phone. You do not need to say you're sorry.

You have visited your son once. How did that go? He took you to Paris—how terribly generous of him. Did you go there in the spring? Did you have to avert your eyes many times? Is your son single? Oh, he got married last year. Congratulations. You do not look pleased about that. May I say that your soured look adds years to your face, ma'am? He got married to a foreigner, you say. A white girl. Does she not come under the umbrella of the Abrahamic faiths? Is she not equipped with a good moral compass? That does not matter, you say. Did your son and this girl he fell in love with seek premarital counseling? Did they discuss religious and cultural boundaries, children of varying hues, the difficulty of trying forever to stand on the narrow strip of common ground between them? Oh dear, you showed him pictures of nice, sensible girls from your own country, and he rejected all of them? You are worried that the white girl's way of cooking a curry is too different from yours. Please write down the names of your son and daughter-in-law here, from left to right, then from right to left. Mm-oh-sin. You see how I slowed down there to catch that tricky *h* sound. Emma. That is a wholesome name. How shrunken it looks in your script. I shall keep this paper for my records.

It says here that you first went to the U.S. three years ago. When you were on the plane, did you feel an indescribable closeness with fellow passengers who looked and sounded like you? Did you, in certain moments during the journey, think that you were all flying to save relationships with your children? After you entered the airport together, did your brown skins dilute until you were scattered specks among lighter shades? Did you and your husband have to hold each other's hands to reassure yourselves of your legitimate existences? Was the effort to speak in English too much to bear? Ah, you kept slipping into your mother tongue! That must have resulted in some confusion and mild terror. Did Americans sound like they do on TV shows? Do I look like a person from a sitcom?

You say you really like my country, sir. Yes, it is a beautiful place, for the most part. Yes, the malls are big and the roads are wide and there is law and order—for the most part. The lawns have sprinklers, and fair-skinned children, who are the picture of health, ride their bicycles after school. And there is food, yes, so much food. You were impressed by how people didn't give your foreign outfits a second glance? Being politely ignored can be a comfort sometimes, I agree. You say that you found yourself pleasantly unafraid when going to your place of worship. You found Americans most kind when your daughter asked for help with the car when it broke down on the way to the mosque. When you reached there, did you and the others like you congregate like lost birds? Did you seek out histories similar to yours in the lines of other faces? Did you warm your hands in theirs and they in yours as you exchanged the names of the cities you were from? Did the aching muscle of your tongue relax as it stretched itself into familiar words?

Can you please write, in your own pretty letters, "How do you do?" and the answer to that, "I am fine, thank you!"? Yes, I have tried to learn to say these sounds, but the "ha" sticks in my throat and I cannot say "kha" without sounding like I need respiratory assistance. Oh, you are pointing at your throat, ma'am. Now you sound like you are choking. Sir, please pat your wife on her back just in case. Thank you.

Has your daughter ever left the comfort of her home to make a trip back here? Once, you say, two years ago. She had a big red suitcase and half of it was full of gifts—you recall this so fondly.

Sweaters and shirts for her father, shoes and scarves for her mother. A new watch and a bottle of perfume for each. She once said that the heat and the chaos in the city of her birth were stifling her? Perhaps she really meant your home but kept that thought locked up. Perhaps she was reminded of things she'd rather forget. When my wife and I go back, we'll leave behind things we'd rather not remember. No, ma'am, I cannot disclose to you where in the States we will return to. I must remind you that I'm the only one allowed to ask questions here. I shall make a note of your interest in my future whereabouts. Please wipe off your look of alarm and stop digging your fingers into your husband's arm. This is merely common procedure.

I must commend you on your neat handwriting. You say you filled out both applications all by yourself, sir. Did your wife not fill her own form? Oh, she signed her name in her own hand. Could you not trust her to not make mistakes? Did you stand behind her, breathing down her neck, to make sure her trembling signature was on the line? My wife writes letters every day. There are piles of them on a corner of our table, waiting to be sent. And she has beautiful handwriting, too. I think she writes to old school friends and to people who have moved away. For a while, she wrote to my mother and my mother wrote back. I did not read those letters. When we spend time together, we talk about the parks we will visit and the wildlife we'll see and the food we'd like to eat in each state back home.

How long has it been since you last saw your son? He visited here with his wife a few months ago—is she terribly British? Did she try at all to soften her clipped accent when talking to you? Was she willing to stand by your son through thick and thin, in a way worthy of a love song from the West? Was she unnerved by the calls to prayer five times a day? You say she managed to learn a few words in your language and wore the clothes you grudgingly bought for her. You say you held your breath and watched her face the whole time she was in your home. You are looking old again, ma'am. When you waved goodbye to your son at the airport, did your heart turn over in your chest? Did you stay awake that night wondering if you'd waved to her, too? Was your last thought, before sleep came, of their possible children? You say you have already picked out their names in your head.

You know that you will not understand what your grand-children will say, and they will not understand your nostalgia, your sentimentality, your wrinkled wish to hear them talk in your native tongue.

My wife says she would like our child—should we miraculously be blessed with one—to have many children. Sometimes I worry that I don't want a child as much as she does. She wears long shirts and loose pants and sits in meditation. My mother took to wearing floral blouses when she moved to Florida. It's what everyone wore there, she said.

I see you own a house here. Is that the place where everything started going wrong with your children, even as they were driven to private schools and back by their chauffeurs? Did you not read the works of great writers from your part of the world to them when they were young? Did you not teach them nuance, syntax, and semantics? You are looking rueful about missed opportunities. I shall make a note of that. You say it is your husband's fault because he installed cable TV. Your daughter learned how to say "yeah" and that there were places in the world with no clamor and humidity, and your son learned that he needed pocket money. Sir, please do not shush your wife. Everything is relevant.

Is your house big and empty now? You say the last time it was full was at your daughter's wedding after which she flew far, far away. Do you have servants to dust all the unused furniture? Do you keep your valuables in the bank? Do you faithfully pay your taxes?

Now, you must answer me truthfully. Remember, if you lie, I will find out. Have you ever been involved in any extreme religious activities? Does your faith not waver? Do you really believe? Do you hold yourself accountable for your sins and mistakes? You say your husband doesn't always say his prayers. Sir, you must understand that this causes your wife pain. Ma'am, don't nag your husband. You wouldn't like to lose him. My wife has a collection of staggeringly beautiful rosaries. She cleans them once a week, then puts them back. I don't know, maybe the colors are spiritual enough for her. Once I held a blue one, but felt nothing.

Do you wear comfortable shoes when traveling? You understand that it is best not to look too different. When walking outside, it is better to talk about the weather, your grandchildren, what you'd like for lunch. It is better to speak in English, no matter how broken. You're always fingerprinted at the airport, you say? That is just part of normal procedure, sir. We all take our shoes and belts off, we all put our hands up in the air and turn ourselves around. Once I was stuck behind a young couple trying to fold their baby's stroller so it could go on the scanner belt. The baby was squalling and the mother looked terrible and the father was muttering. So you see, sir, you cannot really complain.

Why do you think you should be given the visas? Is it really right to encourage this system of borders, of suspicion? Shouldn't we all be one big family on earth? You look unsure about the right answer to this one. Well, I, for one, like everything to be in its own tidy little space. My black socks, blue socks, and gray socks have their own compartments. They do not mingle and they do not get lost. I believe we're of the same mind there, you and me. I shall make a note of that.

You say you miss your daughter and grandchildren terribly, even the as-yet-unborn one. Does your daughter send you flowers on your birthday or at least leave a special message on the phone? She takes out time for you every Friday, I see. In what language does she bring up past grievances? Your relationship is improving with the passage of time, you say. I hope she knows that you are already old, and your fingers tremble a little, and your hair under your scarf is very gray.

Do you have health insurance? Have you imagined having a heart attack in a foreign country? Have you planned the necessary conversations in multiple languages? Do you think your son and his wife will take the first flight out to see you? Would they remember the words of the prayers that would have to be said? It would be a glorious thing if you caused the whole family to be reunited on American soil. A departure that would stay in the hearts long after you're gone. You look pale, sir. I don't fear death myself, though I would prefer an instant one and I would prefer to have it in the U.S. It would mean less paperwork for my wife.

I don't know what to make of my wife's choices in clothes and the glittering rosaries and the drifty look on her face. They all confuse me. Sometimes I think I made a mistake bringing us here. But the good news is that, in a couple of months, we pack up and go back to the States. My term here is almost at an end. It will be nice to be home again, where addresses have zip codes and kids sell lemonade and there's baseball on TV, even though I do not like baseball.

When you have been away for too long, do you miss the names of your streets? Do you look at clear skies and miss the fumes and the smells and the sheer noise of this city? Do you miss walking to the mosque with other retired men? Is it too quiet for you in the homes of your children sometimes because they are inexplicably busy? Do you follow the news from home? You are always up-to-date, I see. I suppose you would like to move out of your country, this country, wouldn't you? Your children enjoy first-world comforts—why not make your own twilight years easy? You could find a section of a city where others like you live largely out of sight. My mother gave up on the cold Chicago winters after her second husband died. When she got to Florida, she said she should've gone there sooner.

She worried about my safety when I told her I was moving all the way here, said she was sure to see my face on TV one of these days, dead in a bomb explosion. She slipped on a bar of soap in the shower and died. Do you use anti-slip mats? You must. Tell your daughter and your son to use them, as well as their spouses. Even the ones you don't like.

You say you would really rather continue living here than anywhere else. I see you are shrugging your shoulders and smiling in a self-conscious way. There is no need to be embarrassed, sir. We can't help our preference for the place we'd rather be when watching TV in the evening. And if we're lucky, that's where we get to be buried.

I think my mother liked Florida. She made eight new friends in her first month there. She never had cholesterol problems or blood pressure problems. She had a loud voice. She might have been singing when she slipped and fell and died. I only ever saw her condo in a picture she sent me. She was standing in front of it in a pink and green shirt. No, you may not ask what her name was. Look how the sun has slipped lower in the sky and made the room's fluorescent lights brighter. Your skin and lips appear dry through the Plexiglas. Is that why you take off your glasses and rub your eyes, sir?

When I am back where I come from, will my wife and I look at the news on the TV and exclaim, "We know that place!"? Will the colors on the screen remind her briefly of her rosaries, tossed somewhere among a jumble of other things she doesn't need in the room she had started to paint baby blue but stopped?

And when you are back here where you come from, will you wonder out loud several times a day that the taxi cabs look so different, yet they all drive the same way? Will you hope the phone rings, so you can tell this to your son or daughter? Will you eat your food with your fingers and I with a spoon? Will you remember that the s is silent in "Illinois," and will I forget the word for horse in your language? Will I remember that one evening when I sat working late, a janitor bought me a samosa and a Pepsi? Will you remember the lady in your daughter's neighborhood who welcomed you with a plate of peanut butter cookies? If we see one another again, on whose land will it be?

LOVED ONES

SO NOW HERE THEY all were. *It was almost like a line from a song*, thought Zara. Her palms were not clammy, but her mouth was dry. And she was OK. She was OK. She felt the weight of her daughter Sana on her right arm, and, after a moment, decided that she was not uncomfortable with it. And when Leena, who was four, squeezed into the space between her back and the sofa, Zara was OK with that, too. She closed her eyes and felt her body thrum with the relief of these realizations. Her children smelled of biscuits, dipped in tea, and grass. She took in these scents, and her happiness flew up and stood dangerously on one foot of a cliff's edge. It was almost too much to bear.

Almost half an hour ago, when Hassan had stopped the car in front of his mother's house, her legs had suddenly felt heavy.

"I'm going to wait here for a while," she said, trying to sound lighthearted even as the smell of polish from the dashboard increased her discomfort.

"Did you take your medicine?" he asked, his tone quick.

"Yes, of course." But the doubt and rising panic were easy to hear in her statement.

Hassan shook his head. "Do you have it with you?"

The speed of her movements matching the clip of his words, Zara pulled a small jar out of her bag and popped it open. Hassan was already holding up a takeaway cup. "It's not that old," he said. Zara swallowed her pills with the remainder of coffee long gone cold.

And now here were her bare feet on the blue, blue carpet. Mrs. Diwan preferred that people leave their shoes at the entrance. Zara's children looked chubbier, and combed, and shiny. Of course she wasn't afraid to see them. Was it four weeks? Or five? Thinking about that was difficult and she made that thought become as small as a dot, then smaller, until she couldn't see it anymore. She chewed on a piece of loose skin on her thumb and considered saying something to Mrs. Diwan, who sat straight and smiled stiffly from the other side of the carpet.

"Did you have a nice stay?" Mrs. Diwan asked.

Zara tried to discreetly pick the piece of thumb skin off her tongue, while nodding vigorously. "Yes, they were very nice there. It was lovely."

"Lovely," Mrs. Diwan repeated. "I'm glad you enjoyed it."

Was it lovely? Zara wondered. *It must have been.* She had a residual impression of the retreat as a place full of women who moved slowly and sat slowly and got up slowly to the sound of the lapping of water somewhere. Almost like a spa, only with doctors. One of them had told her, on the day she was leaving, "You *will* be greeted by loved ones." She wasn't sure if the doctor really had emphasized the word "will." Zara fixed her teeth onto a new piece of skin. Next to her, Hassan and the girls talked about many, many things. She didn't feel compelled to pay attention to their words. Just the sound of their chatter was enough, for now.

The doors in the other side of the room slid open and a young girl entered. Nazish, Zara remembered. Cautiously, Nazish pushed a serving trolley, the cups, bowls and spoons rattling as the wheels transitioned from cold floor to soft carpet. A big brown dupatta lay over half of her head and draped her front, the ends falling behind her. Zara saw her slowly, slowly come closer. Sana and Leena jumped down from the sofa and ran to the cupcakes with yellow frosting. *How strange all this is*, Zara thought. Hassan filled their plates with whatever they asked for. An old habit made Zara want to tell them they were never going to eat all of that, but she felt shy. One of the girls said something and it made Hassan laugh. He sat on the carpet with them. *Crisscross applesauce*, she thought. *Like in their school.* Nazish stood behind the trolley, hands clasped in front. Zara knew the girl was staring at her.

The car ride to her mother-in-law's house had been long. Zara had looked out of the window at the old trees under which stood vendors with carts, and when they stopped at a traffic light, she bought a comb from a child who was selling cheap plastic wares. His serious face appeared in the side mirror as the car moved forward.

"Have they been going to school?" she asked, and Hassan answered in the affirmative.

"Did they ask about me?" and Hassan told her they had asked about her every day, and that they had not been worried because they knew she would be coming back soon. And wasn't she happy going back?

"I'm happy," she said, still looking out of her window. She worried that she'd bought only one comb for her two children.

Later, after Nazish wheeled away the trolley with its little treats, they brought the girls home with them. "I'm taking them back today" is what Hassan had said to his mother. They stood in a triangle and Zara pressed her feet upon the softness of the carpet. Mrs. Diwan's mouth was a thin line, her arms crossed over her chest. Zara looked down and marveled at how clean it looked; maybe the girls' grandmother had been strict about them eating in this room. Mrs. Diwan opened her mouth and closed it. Then, as if she had settled an argument in her head, she said, "Fine. But Nazish goes with you." That's how they drove home, five instead of four.

"We'll have to tell Nazish," Zara said to Hassan that night, a familiar anxiety filling her stomach. She wished she had spoken up and told her mother-in-law that she did not need her maid, but she was so deep under the mound of debt of Hassan's Tolerance of Zara that acquiescing to his mother allowed her to repay him a little.

"She probably already knows," he said with a sigh. Zara felt him watching her as she stared at the ceiling and nibbled at her finger. He was tired, she could tell; he'd had to drive all over the city and now, finally, the pieces of his family were back where they belonged. "Goodnight," he said, and turned his back to her. Zara tried to remember if it was five weeks or six. Things looked a little unfamiliar in her house.

In the morning, she woke up early and happy. The house was quiet, but outside there were crows. Zara stepped onto the grass, dew-covered blades touching her feet through the open spaces in her sandals. She breathed in and out and smelled the warmth of the summer. She glanced at the trees that had grown up around the perimeter of the lawn. There was no subtlety in the red-orange blooms among the leaves, and they caused a part of her mind some disquiet—small windows opened into tunnels leading to other similar trees and yellow afternoons from long ago.

Zara went inside to the kitchen and opened all the cupboards and the fridge. Nothing had changed. She would make breakfast, a big one. Pancakes for Sana and Leena, and an omelet for Hassan with tomatoes and onions in it, the way he liked. When Nazish came in to help, Zara told her that she was managing fine on her own. The girl was reluctant to leave and stood by the door. Zara opened and shut drawers.

"Where are the knives?" she asked.

Nazish shrugged. She'd never worked in this house before. "Baji, ab aap theek ho gaee ho?" she asked. *Baji, are you cured now?*

Zara frowned and told her to find something else to do, but she said this in a low voice. Unhurriedly, Nazish went away, playing with the ends of her dupatta. After breakfast, Zara took a glass of water to her room and shook two pink pills from a jar. It was easy to swallow them; each was only as big as the nail on her little finger.

"Today was a good day," she told Hassan later that night. She had not wanted to hurry away from her children's bedsides; she had stayed, reading them story after story until her voice became hoarse. Then Leena had wanted her mother not to leave the room, so Zara had lain next to her on the narrow bed, half of her body on its wooden frame, and that had not bothered her.

Hassan closed his laptop and turned to her. She knew he had been told by her doctor to do that when she spoke to him, that it would help them to talk and listen better.

"We played games and colored, and Leena sat on my lap and ate her lunch," Zara went on. Then she remembered about the knives and asked Hassan if he knew where they were. She suddenly felt embarrassed and said, "I need them for making food." She did not look at him.

"Can't Nazish do the cooking? She can do a good job, Ammi said."

"You know I've been good with my pills." It was true. In the morning, Hassan had tipped the little pills out onto the table and counted them. She hadn't given him any cause to worry.

He smiled and said, "Let's go."

They walked to the kitchen. She looked away when he reached over the top of a cabinet and pulled toward him—slowly, for there were knives and scissors in it—a heavy shoebox. It made a rasping sound against the dust and increased Zara's discomfort.

"I could've climbed up onto the counter and gotten them, you know," she said, trying to make light of the moment.

Changing his grip on the edge of the box, Hassan lifted it down. The edge slid out from between his fingers and tipped forward, the knives and scissors falling. Zara screamed and

Hassan swore and pushed her out of the way. But it was already over. The instruments lay on the counter and the floor, inert once more. Hassan picked them up and threw them into the box. "You're bleeding," Zara said. There was a thin line of blood from a cut on the back of his right hand. "Don't get it on the counter."

When they woke up the next day, Sana and Leena made a big fuss over their father's Band-Aid. They put their arms around his neck and hugged him. They told him that they did not want to go to school. Zara watched him give them piggyback rides up to their room. She stood at the bottom of the stairs, listening to their shrieks of laughter. Then Leena appeared at the top, in her school uniform, asking her mother to play with them, and Zara felt relief massage away the worry from her brain. She asked, "Do you like my shirt?" smoothing down the yellow fabric of her qameez. Leena said that yellow was her favorite color and Zara trembled with joy. She thought about tomorrow and all the days to come, saw herself poised on the edge of a new beginning, shiny with promise. Things were different now.

On weekday mornings, Hassan left with the girls to take them to school before going to work, and Zara walked from room to room, putting away toys and books and crayons. Nazish stayed in the kitchen, sitting on the floor. She hadn't yet been asked to do anything in the house.

She did not clean the tiles or make meals or wipe the counters, and she didn't seem worried about the lack of things to do. Sometimes Zara heard her humming quietly. After some time, she found it easier to give the maid small tasks, found herself feeling better for it because when Nazish was scrubbing a floor, it did not matter so much what she knew about Zara. Soon, the maid didn't have time to sit on the floor and daydream. Zara started taking her medicine in the morning, after which she went to bed and slept until noon. She always woke up covered in sweat, so she showered and wore bright colors before leaving with the driver to pick up Sana and Leena from school. She stayed in the car because the entrance of the school building was crowded with other parents she used to talk to.

Most nights she was able to fall asleep and stay asleep, but one time she woke up and was disappointed to see that it was only three in the morning. Her face and back and armpits were slick with sweat, and there was a gnawing hunger in her stomach. For just a moment, she thought she was still at her retreat, where the doors were made of deodar wood and the floors of marble. There was a manmade pond, but she could never find where it was. She breathed in deeply and remembered that she was on her bed in her house, but a part of her memory snagged on a face in a room. It belonged to a woman sitting on a soft, beige leather sofa. Zara couldn't remember her name. The woman had a smile that invited confidences.

"Have you been here a long time?" she began.

"Maybe three or four weeks," Zara said, willing her voice to sound more certain.

"Have you found what you were looking for?" The woman tapped a pen against an open notebook on her lap.

Zara shook her head. "I wasn't looking for anything."

"Your husband didn't take care of you."

"No! He was wonderful!"

"You hated your children?"

Zara felt guilty, but she knew this was not true. "They are all wonderful. It was only me, always."

The woman laughed. She put the notebook and pen on a table and said, "Let's go walk in the garden before Dr. Hena finds us here." They went to the door and she turned to Zara and said with a grin, "You did well. We must play this again."

Zara looked at the clock and saw that it was almost four. She was relieved to find herself sleepy again.

When the heat turned stickier and the sun yellower, staying out for longer, Zara wondered if she should stop taking the pink pills entirely. They were making it hard for her to fit into her clothes, and the coldest setting on the air-conditioner was not enough to stop the dampness from covering her face. And she was happy now, wasn't she? So she opened the jars one by one and flushed away their contents.

One afternoon, during her daughters' summer holidays, they went to the park. Nazish played with Leena and Sana while Zara watched from a bench. Papery blossoms from trees lay on the grass. Down there, underneath her feet, they were harmless. Sweat gathered quickly on her upper lip and she wiped it off with her sleeve. There was no breeze and she wondered how all the other women were able to walk on the 350-meter-long jogging track in their shalwar qameez. She thought their sneakers looked comical. A younger woman came running up the track, effortlessly flying past the walkers in her pink and black running shoes. Two little boys called out "Mama" to her from the swings and she waved to them, and Zara felt self-conscious about the bulges under her shirt.

The heat pressed up her nostrils, went down into her lungs. She watched Nazish's eyes widen in admiration at the runner. A second later, Sana and Leena started arguing and their high-pitched voices fell loudly on her eardrums. Nazish went to mediate and soon the girls were laughing again. Zara thought that the dupatta on Nazish's head looked slovenly, sitting on her frizzy hair, so far away from her forehead.

At home in the kitchen, Nazish got busy making sand-wiches, noisily setting out plates and cups on the table. She was in the mood to have a friendly chat, Zara sitting at the kitchen table.

"You used to be like that running woman, baji, before you had babies," she said. "My sister has always looked the same, though. After she had her baby, she used to cry all day and not feed it." Nazish twisted open a packet of bread, the red plastic crackling. "Her husband gave the baby to his mother and kicked my sister out of the house. Your husband is a good man."

Zara looked away from Nazish. Leena and Sana whined that they did not want to eat. Their voices were too thin. Zara picked up a glass and threw it to the floor, and the room was finally quiet. She locked herself in her bathroom and climbed into the empty tub. Hours later, Hassan knocked on the door, but she came out only when she heard him walk away. She went quietly to the children's room and found them asleep. She lay down next to Sana and whispered to her that she was sorry. Then she went to Leena and kissed her forehead and said sorry to her as well. She was going to give them a perfect day tomorrow. She stayed in their room and fell asleep there.

Mrs. Diwan came over with a woman called Nilofer on a Monday afternoon. Nazish carried in samosas, cake, and tea on a tray. Zara smiled at her mother-in-law's friend and wondered who she was. Mrs. Diwan talked about a charity dinner she had attended last week, and when Leena came into the room, she allowed herself to be led away by her. Zara and Nilofer were left alone in the drawing room.

"Would you like to see a baby turtle?" Zara asked.

Nilofer smiled and set her plate down on the coffee table. She delicately wiped her fingers clean with a tissue. "I would love to."

Upstairs in the girls' room was a tank, filled with water which appeared slightly green.

Zara and Nilofer peered into it. A little turtle, no longer than half a forefinger, sat on a rock.

"Do you know anything about turtles?" Zara asked. The stillness of the water in the tank made her speak almost in a whisper.

"I've never had pets," Nilofer replied. The look on her face made it clear she found the creature's little face repulsive.

"I bought him last week as a surprise for my children." Zara tapped the glass softly.

"He's not looking so well." Nilofer cleared her throat. "Try giving him some vitamins, maybe?"

Zara wondered if the turtle was going to move into the water soon. "Who the hell are you?" she asked quietly.

Nilofer saw the turtle's wrinkled eyelid move down, then up. A slow blink. "I help people," she said. "Do you know, I'd never seen a real turtle before."

Zara wanted to rub the turtle's shell but he looked like he was almost asleep.

"When we count our blessings every day, we start healing our hearts," said Nilofer, breathing out each word. "I keep a gratitude journal."

It was Saturday morning. Zara was going to the house of an old friend who was collecting donations to send to earthquake victims in northern Pakistan. Winter was coming and warm clothes were scarce. When Zara received the text message the day before, she wanted to reply, but she'd fallen out of the habit of staying in touch. By nighttime, she had almost emptied her part of the big cupboard that she shared with Hassan. She had four big plastic bags' worth of clothes and shoes to give. She felt buoyed by selflessness, happy even, and wrote back to her friend that she would like to help. And when, in return, she was told that they all missed her, Zara felt flooded with the feeling of being wanted, and she chastised herself for not telling her close friend that she had needed to go to a special place that she called a retreat. Her fingers typed, forming sentences for confidential sharing, feeling cheerful about the sadness in her mind. Still, she did not say that she'd had to go away for a while. She did say that she was good now, better.

Now Zara was on her way; she had not wanted to go with the driver. While she'd been saying goodbye to her children and telling them that she would be back soon, she'd seen Hassan look for her jar of medicine. At a red light, she stopped and carefully examined the hopeful feeling inside her. The pavement looked as if it needed to sleep for a few hours more, but the trees standing tall behind the walls of houses were more awake. Zara turned off the air-conditioning and rolled down the window. She waited for the light to change. The smell of grass and, from the branches of a tree, the sound of a koel drifted in. Its coos marked the air with thin curves and an unbearable sadness spread through Zara. Dew and grass and koels—the vignettes arranged themselves rapidly in a spiral, spinning dizzyingly to an unseen center. Her mouth felt dry and she wondered if there was something to eat or drink in the car. She found a box of apple juice with a chewed-up straw. The juice tasted warm and sharp, zinging over her tongue, but she finished it. Somebody behind her honked a horn. It was time to move on. She glanced in the rearview mirror and the car behind her was too close. The man driving it wore sunglasses and, for ten seconds, she wondered if he wanted her dead, but then he changed lanes and sped away.

"I can't stay long, Amber," Zara said to her friend.

They were in Amber's garage, a third of which was full of boxes and bags, some labeled neatly, others hastily closed. Amber crouched in front of the boxes, peering into them and then writing "clothes," "toys," or "misc" on their sides.

"I asked people to sort out what they were giving but you know how they can get, right, they think donating is a chance to do a little decluttering." Amber shook her head. "Anyway, what have you been up to? I haven't seen you at all these past few months." She lifted a plastic carrier bag and relocated it, setting it down before Zara could move to help.

Zara wanted to leave. "I've just been busy with some things in the family," she said.

Maybe Amber had not read her message last night. She felt foolish for having sent out such quantities of herself.

"I read what you wrote," Amber said, putting the lid on her marker. "I wish you'd told me sooner. You shouldn't keep things like that bottled up inside. You know, when I see these piles and piles of clothes, I feel that I can't even understand what being blessed means. I mean, these are our *extras* and there are cold and hungry people out there for whom these will be *essentials*. We are so lucky, Zara. We have no room for sadness."

"I am not good for the children, I shouldn't be here," Zara said to Hassan that night. She was crying, but not noisily. She nibbled at a piece of skin until it broke away, leaving all of her finger smooth. "What shall I do?"

"I don't know," Hassan said, sitting up on his side of the bed. "I don't know, *I don't know, I don't know*," his voice rising with every repetition. He took ten loud, deep breaths. "You're not taking your medication anymore, are you?"

"It was making me feel ill." Her voice was thick with tears. He walked out of the room. She heard him climb onto the counter in the kitchen and put the knives on top of the cabinet. He did not come back to the room. After a while, Zara got up from the bed and went to sleep on the carpet in Leena and Sana's room.

"Look at that," she said.

"Look at what?" he asked.

"That building over there, with the pink shirt on the balcony."

He glanced at the pink shirt at the end of her fingertip. "You like that building?"

"It's beautiful. It doesn't belong here."

"Well. It's housing for people."

She thought his sentence was foolish, and perhaps he thought the same because when the light turned green, he pressed hard on the accelerator and she moved back with a jerk. When they reached home, she waited to see if he would stride ahead without her. She felt waves of gratitude when he opened her car door, and she asked him if he wanted some coffee, worried that he would say no, that he would tell her he hated her because they had just taken their daughters back to his mother's house. "Coffee would be great," he said. She made it in his favorite cup and put three cookies next to it. She saw that he had gone to the bathroom, so she put the cup down on the table and sat on a chair. She could hear the shower and wondered if he was really just reading on the edge of the bathtub. She rapped sharply on the door and asked him if he was OK. He yelled back cheerfully that he would be done in a minute. When he came out, she took the towel from him, her fingers checking for genuine dampness. It smelled of soap, and that made her think of her children. Her mouth turned down at the corners.

She said, "Let's get Sana and Leena back from your mother's. I'll start my medication again. I'll start a whole new bottle. But not Nazish; I don't want her. I only want the children."

Hassan stood, sipped his now-cold coffee, and said politely, "They need to grow up in a normal environment. Maybe after you are back from the retreat."

Zara swallowed and nodded and frowned in a grown-up, understanding sort of way to show her husband that they were making a decision together for their children's betterment, the way regular couples decide about schools and extracurricular activities. She understood that she had failed to give her family perfect days and that it was indelicate to tell a person with her condition that she had failed. So she made a great show of packing her best clothes and not forgetting her makeup, and after her husband turned his back to her and went to sleep, she sat on her side of the bed all night, waiting for the morning.

BELIEVERS

AFTER GUL HIT THE little Suzuki with his truck, sending it spinning—possibly killing the man who had been driving it—he told himself, *I need to stop.* When he finally pressed the brake he had traveled a few kilometers away from the car. He got out and gulped the cool night air, nausea rising in his gullet. The other drivers would be here in a moment; he could hear their trucks coming up the road behind him. Would Amir and Farooq want to take him to the police? Would Hasan agree with them?

When the men arrived and got out of their trucks, Gul watched them warily. Hasan stayed in the darkness, and for a moment Gul wanted to rush to him and offer to give up his salary for a year. But then Amir lit a cigarette and Farooq did the same, offering another one to Gul, and he took it gratefully. They stood in the yellow of the headlights, their hands shaking as they put the tips to their mouths. Farooq, his voice wobbly, said whoever was in that car was fine, probably—there was no fire, no smoke. And why had that bastard been going the wrong way anyway? Amir said it was the fault of the highway authority for not putting up clear signs. Farooq said he knew a man who had survived a motorbike accident without a single scratch on his body only to die of a gunshot wound the next week, and Amir said it was all qismat how these things happened.

Gul ignored their nervous chatter. He knew they didn't want to be here, where they could be implicated in the accident. They stayed because they knew Hasan wanted them to stay. Hasan had given them their jobs transporting dried fruits and nuts between cities. He gave them their earnings, which were more generous than what other truckers got. He gave them holidays and bonuses on Eid. He had a few rules—there were never to be more than three other drivers in the group, and every now and then they had to travel together on the highway. He told them he would take care of them as long as they did exactly what he said.

Gul looked at Hasan. Why was he standing by himself? Why wasn't he here, telling him what he was supposed to do? Gul remembered an afternoon from a year ago. Hasan bought all of them tea. When he left, Farooq leaned forward and said, "Child, there are things you don't know about that man. It's not always wholesome goods he takes about. Not just pistachios and almonds." He said the names almost mockingly. "He's clever. It's always small things mixed up with everything else." Amir nodded.

"What kind of things?" Gul asked, but only because he wanted to know more about Hasan, just like he wanted to know where he got his haircut from or what kind of cologne he wore.

"Foreign cigarettes, gutka. Soaps."

"Soaps." Gul smiled.

"You won't think it's so funny when the police catch on."

"You don't seem too worried to me."

Amir said, "See, none of us know exactly what we're transporting or when we're transporting it. And it's harder for the police to track him when there's a group of us together. But we keep our distance from him. And you should do the same."

Farooq brought his face so close Gul could smell the tea on the older man's breath. "Trust us, we've known him a lot longer than you have."

But over the last year, Hasan's kindness to Gul had mattered far more to him than the words of those men. Hasan was thoughtful. Sometimes he gave Gul four or five hundred extra rupees, out of sight of the others, saying that a young boy should have fun. A lot of times, he paid for Gul's dinner, making sure he didn't go to sleep less than full.

Standing on the side of the road, Gul's stomach twisted into knots. *I've disappointed God*, he thought. *And I've disappointed Hasan*. He saw Hasan walk toward his truck, and his thin body shivered. The other men stopped talking. Hasan moved his fingers slowly over the dent in the corner. He looked at Gul. "You didn't get hurt anywhere, did you?" Gul shook his head.

"Were you going fast?"

"No."

He couldn't tell Hasan the truth, that he knew nothing about the moments before the impact. He had been asleep in his seat, his hands on the steering wheel. His eyes had flown open only at the moment of collision to see the car ricochet off to the side, and the shape of a man strike the windshield. Would Hasan punish him by taking away the key and his protection, and leave him by the road?

Once, Hasan had found Gul playing cards with some men, a fifty-rupee note in front of him. Eyes wide with fury, Hasan tore the note in half. Gul scrambled after him, saying he would never gamble again. He said Hasan was like a father to him, and he began to weep when Hasan spat on the ground and said he wasn't anybody's damned father. But Hasan also hadn't left. When Gul stopped crying, Hasan said, "I never saw mine, and you hardly saw yours. Which makes us the same kind of person, do you see? Those men you were with, they're done with their lives. Finished. But not you."

Hasan glanced at Gul's truck one last time and said, "It's best if we move away from here. Best not to get involved. Nobody would care who was going the wrong way or the right way. We're just truckers." He said it like a plain fact, no bitterness in his voice. Gul felt his knees weaken; Hasan was not going to abandon him.

Gul started the engine of his truck—did not look in the rearview mirror—and drove off. Only when there was a merciful curve in the highway did he allow himself to relax a little. He felt a twinge of hunger.

For ten whole minutes he managed to keep his thoughts away from the dead man, but his brow continued to sweat even as he tried to wipe it dry with his sleeve. "There is such a thing as destiny," he said out loud. That man in the car, it had been his time to die. Gul's truck was just the means. Had God ordained that the man was to die by slipping on a bar of soap and cracking his head on the floor, nobody would have blamed the soap. Men who killed with intent were a different kind of creature. Like Murtaza, who had strangled the man who had hurt his sister. Or Juman, who had shot his uncle seven times for stealing from their shop.

Gul's own mother had been a big believer in qismat. When Gul's father divorced her and moved to the city, Gul asked his mother to get him back, but she said, "I can't stand in the way of what's been ordained." And when a letter came from his father with the news that he had married again, Gul watched, astonished, as his mother folded up the letter into a small square and tucked it into her purse instead of tearing it up. A year later his father was run over by a bus and, to Gul's disgust, his mother actually cried and told him to read the Quran and say a prayer for his dead father to go to heaven. Gul had only pretended to do so, refusing to give this bit of help to his father.

When Gul was ten and they had to leave their small, one-room house because they didn't have money for rent, his mother had shrugged and said, "It is God's will." When monsoon rains flooded their second home, she said it was as God wanted. When she was fired from one of her jobs as a housemaid because the employer thought she had stolen money, Gul's mother had said it was all destiny.

"But look," she said to him that night after he complained about having to eat plain dal and roti again, "we have a roof over our heads, and you go to school."

"And?" Gul had asked, bitterness on his young tongue.

"And I have two arms and you have two arms. I have two legs and so do you." She had gone on and on, and he had fallen asleep to the sound of countless blessings.

When she died, she left him with envelopes full of currency notes in a tied-up plastic bag and their unpainted, two-room house. He sold the house to the first willing buyer, added the money to the bag, and put it under the floor mat of his truck. He didn't tell anyone about it or take any of it out. Not even to pay back Hasan, who had lent him cash for the funeral. Hasan had never asked Gul how much he'd made from the sale of the little house.

Suddenly Gul felt a bit better and pushed a cassette into the player. This would be his last overnight delivery job, he decided. He would use the cash to make a down payment for a rickshaw, or one of those old, black Corolla taxis. He had heard that taxi drivers could make five thousand rupees a day, and they got to sleep through the night, away from the moonlight. He thought it strange how it was shining over his truck at the same time as it was over his mother's grave. He imagined it lighting up the broken glass of the car, the corpse of that man. Who would worry about him first? Did he have a brother or a wife who would tell the police that their beloved was missing? What if he had nobody? The unclaimed body would lie undisturbed for days and days, getting covered up with dust. An automatic burial.

Tiredness swept over Gul. He thought, *This has happened to you because you are not a good person.* The singer's voice in the small cab of the truck began to make him feel ill, and he punched the stop button. He would have to go back. Everything would go wrong if he didn't; his bag of money would become a burden, he would lose his friendship with Hasan, perhaps even the use of his legs. Punishment could strike from unexpected places.

He glanced into the mirror. There were no vehicles on the road. Amir and Farooq must have sped ahead some time ago. Was Hasan still somewhere far behind? Gul drove his truck onto the gravel on the roadside and swung it around, his foot on the accelerator. He was going the wrong way now. Dread and adrenaline spurred him on. He muttered, "Come on! Come on!" but the place where he had hit the car didn't appear. What he ought to do, he realized with a rush, was ask God for help. God was going to give him help, Gul thought fiercely, because Gul had good intentions and his god rewarded good intentions. He needed to say a prayer free of worldly concerns, the way his mother had, free of disbelief in destiny, containing only gratitude, repentance—a selfless request. He began mumbling, "Help me, please, I'm sorry," but lines from songs kept coming to his lips: "without you I am as if ash" and "my love left me by the river," and he cursed his tainted plea and started all over again.

And then the wreckage of the car appeared. Gul turned off the engine, and in the silence he looked around. Everything was still. He walked toward the car, his shoes crunching in the dirt, his breath loud in his ear. The car's bonnet had been crushed. The front seats were covered with moonlit glass. A man. Gul moved to him, his stomach turning. Through the open door he saw that the man was a boy of around seventeen. There was blood on his face, dried. His eyes were closed. Gul put a cold, trembling hand on the boy's chest and felt the beating of his heart. With a dry sob, Gul thanked God for giving him a sign that he was maybe forgiven. The boy opened his eyes.

Overwhelmed with remorse and affection, Gul said, "I'll take you to a hospital, OK? My truck is right here."

He put his hands under the boy's arms and began to pull him out of the car. The boy screamed, but Gul didn't stop until he had laid him on the ground. The boy groaned pitifully. Gul wished he had water to give him. He took an end of his qameez, wet it with his spit, and tried to rub some of the dried, red-brown blood from the boy's face, but there were gashes there and Gul stopped, afraid to cause more pain. Then he noticed blood seeping through the fabric of the boy's pants. Panicking, not knowing what to do, he tore off a part of his qameez and began to wrap it around the boy's leg, and when he screamed again, Gul started weeping and said he was sorry, and tied the cloth more gently.

He crouched over the boy, his eyes darting over his body. His hair had a sheen to it; perhaps he had a mother who had oiled it for him before he got into the car. Some strands had become stuck in a cut on his forehead. His left foot was bare. Gul took off his own sandal and tucked the boy's foot into it. Gingerly, Gul put light fingers on the boy's neck; nothing seemed broken. He saw the quick, shallow rise and fall of the boy's chest, and when he touched it, the boy hissed through his teeth. *His ribs are hurt*, Gul realized with horror. The boy began to close his eyes. Gul remembered from somewhere that to stop a dying person from dying it was necessary to keep them awake, so he said, "I'm going to get you something to eat." He sprinted to the truck and brought out some bread. He eased the boy's head onto his lap, broke off a part of the bread, and pushed it through the boy's lips.

"You must eat," he said.

Gul fed him piece after piece, and the boy chewed and swallowed until he turned his head away and sighed.

"What is your name?" Gul asked.

"Ahmed," the boy answered, his voice a croak.

"That is a nice name. Where do you live, Ahmed?"

"Karachi."

"I'm from Karachi, too. I drive that big truck over there."

"You hit my car."

Gul's face turned warm in the darkness. "Yes. I am terribly sorry." He wanted to add that he was sorry he had broken Ahmed's body, but he was too ashamed. "I will get you to a doctor. I will pay all your medical bills." He bit his lips and once again grabbed the boy's arms, squatting behind his head. He thought he could carry him over his shoulder to his truck, but Ahmed screamed and, with a cry, Gul let him go. "I'm sorry," he said. Ahmed began to shiver. Quickly, Gul pulled off his shirt and spread it over him. He took Ahmed's cold hands and rubbed them between his own.

"Do you work?" Gul asked the first thing that came to his mind.

Slowly, Ahmed shook his head.

"My boss's name is Hasan. He's a very good man. He says he will make sure I have enough money by the time I'm twenty-five to have my own house. He even showed me where it will be. He says I won't need to work for anyone; I'll have my own business."

Gul's mother had believed the world was meant to be a place of discomfort, but Hasan disliked moroseness and dressed well. His clothes were made of linen. In winter he wrapped himself in a dark brown shawl of fine wool. He liked to say, "Only sad people like to believe in fate. They enjoy feeling helpless. But a smart man doesn't just let things happen to him. He makes his own fate." Gul tried hard to be that kind of man. Confident and unfazed about life. He didn't want to be like Amir and Farooq. They made him feel uncomfortable with their old, holey sweaters and their talks. Sometimes, temporarily freed from their deliveries and the presence of Hasan, they sat on plastic chairs in small tea shops and gave Gul what they called an education. "Hasan doesn't have a family," Amir said. "Unnatural, if you ask me." Another time Farooq said, "Hasan once almost beat a man to death. Did he ever tell you?"

Gul shrugged irritably. "I can't remember."

The two men, older and broader with faces more lined and whiskered, threw their heads back and laughed and patted his narrow back.

Inwardly he had smirked at their unsuccessful lives. And now here he was, sitting in the dirt, shoeless and shirtless, unable to help this boy. His mother would have called this fate.

Ahmed groaned. His breathing had become slower. Gul was certain that if he moved him, he would kill him. The bare skin on Gul's back prickled in the breeze and his stomach rumbled. He felt lonely and worn out from his efforts at atonement. He wished Hasan would find them. He would know what to do.

"What school do you go to?" Gul asked Ahmed.

The boy didn't say anything. His silence scared Gul.

"I left school at sixteen." He spoke hurriedly. "My mother was so angry. She called me greedy, couldn't understand why I needed money."

She had told him that she'd left her place in the north with the river and the mountain for the smoky density of Karachi, learned how to clean houses—squat-walking and moving a large rag in arcs over floors—so that she could send him to school and give him a good future. "And you want to use my sacrifices to become an all-night trucker," she said in disgust. "Nights are for sleeping, days are for working. Don't mess with God's laws. You don't need to do this."

"You know how much I earned the first time?" Gul said to Ahmed. "Eight thousand rupees. That was just for three trips. When I sent it to my mother she cried because it was too much."

She had called him from the shop near her home. "What will I do with it?"

"Buy some new clothes. Be happy. Stop working."

But she was stubborn. "It is not for me to turn away the gift of an earning."

So Gul told Hasan he wanted to work longer, take all the night journeys the other truckers couldn't do. He wanted to send his mother so much money that she would think God would find her ungrateful and greedy if she kept working. Still, she cleaned houses. On a visit home, he got into a fight with her when he told her he was going to buy them train tickets to visit the place where she had grown up. She said she would never use her son's money for useless pleasures like that. And she got her way, too. She'd died suddenly, he was told later. Her body had been found draped over an upturned bucket, the water from it soaking the front of her shirt and dupatta. When he saw her after she had been readied for burial, he thought she looked worried, as if she was afraid Gul had brought her even more food, food for which she had no space or refrigeration or need.

"Is your mother alive?" Gul asked Ahmed.

The boy licked his lips. "I live with my uncle."

"Is he a good uncle?"

"The best."

The hunger in Gul's stomach became forceful and desperate. He reached over and grabbed the remaining bread from the ground, tearing off a large piece with his teeth. Ahmed began to shiver again.

"I have something to give you," Gul said with his mouth full. "It will be so useful for you. Wait right here." He stood up, his legs cramping, and hobbled to the truck. Inside, he lifted the floor mat and picked up the plastic bag of money. He walked back as fast as he could.

"Here. See what I've got for you." He spoke loudly and shook Ahmed's shoulder.

The boy's eyes opened once again, slowly and heavily. Gul shook the bag and the money inside it rustled. "See how nice it sounds? It's money. And it's all for you. You're going to use it after we're done with the hospital." But Ahmed was already drifting back into sleep.

The sound of a vehicle approaching became louder by degrees, and in another minute the shape of Hasan's truck became clear, coming closer. With a mixture of dread and relief, Gul watched it stop and the door open. When he saw Hasan's face, his doubt went away and he leapt to his feet.

"This is Ahmed. He's hurt badly," he said, his words tumbling out.

"I told you to drive on." Hasan spoke through gritted teeth. His eyes were wide, and his shawl hung off one shoulder. He rubbed his hands through his hair and paced the ground, peering into the darkness around them. "This is not a good situation for us."

"We will only take Ahmed to a hospital and leave. We won't even go inside. Promise."

"The police are probably on their way. We will go in my truck."

Thinking that Hasan had relented, Gul bent toward Ahmed to lift him. But the older man said, "I'm not taking that boy with me."

Gul felt crushed. He was going to have to choose. "I can't leave him. You should go; this was my fault."

"That is not how this works." Hasan spoke loudly and slowly, as if to a child. "We are all mixed up in this now. They find you, they find me, we go to jail." Then he took a deep breath. "You are exhausted. You never had a father to fix your mistakes." He reached inside his qameez and very slowly drew out a gun. "Fathers can do a lot to protect their own," he said, his tone soft, reasonable. "But I wouldn't expect you to know that. You'll just have to trust me."

Once, Hasan had said that he wanted to meet Gul's mother. So, proudly and self-consciously, Gul had brought him home. Hasan had insisted that Gul's mother sit on the charpai and that he was perfectly comfortable on the plastic chair. He called her Ma and spent time explaining how the sacks of dried fruits were arranged in the trucks. "There are hundreds of sacks, Ma. That's our job, taking all that food to warehouses and factories so they can turn them into wonderful things to eat. I am never ashamed to tell people that I am a humble truck driver."

Before leaving, Hasan said, "Ma, I promise I'll watch over Gul."

Now, Hasan said, "You go wait inside my truck. This won't take long."

"Ahmed won't do anything!" Gul licked his lips and found sweat and tears on his tongue. "I don't want you to get in trouble because of me."

Hasan's voice became soft and tinged with sadness. "Maybe I was wrong, Gul; maybe you don't want to be my son. Haven't I taken care of you?"

Gul felt sick with misery. He did want to belong to him; there was nobody else. But below him lay the boy. If he died, it would be because of Gul; he would become a murderer. There would be no more heaven, no more meeting his mother.

Hasan pointed the gun at Ahmed. "You're trying to protect the wrong thing, Gul. This boy isn't a part of our plan."

With his free hand, he tried to push Gul away. Then he squeezed the trigger.

Gul heard the shot, but he had moved before the sound, his body covering Ahmed's. If Hasan shouted in surprise, or if Ahmed groaned, he didn't hear it. In the moments before the bullet tore into him, a memory played in his mind: once, Gul had shyly asked Hasan if he wanted to say the morning prayer with him, and Hasan laughed and said he had a different way of beating his devils. He told Gul to hurry and finish his prayer on time, and then he stretched out on the ground, chewing on a stalk of grass.

THE EFFECT OF HEAT
ON POOR PEOPLE

SABA WAS BEGINNING TO think that Kamil was a belligerent man. When she'd married him, she'd known that there wasn't going to be a honeymoon—his financial circumstances didn't permit extravagances—but she wished they could put some neutral space between them. They had each taken three days off from work after the wedding, and, in the hours and weekends that they had to spend together, they discovered they had precious little in common. After the forced post-wedding holiday, they gratefully fell back into their jobs. Saba was a receptionist in an office building, and Kamil was a reporter for an English newspaper. Because they had seen their parents, uncles and aunts, and older cousins make the best of bad relationships, they stumbled along, clumsily.

Saba couldn't understand how Kamil could sound angry about things that excited him. One Saturday afternoon in June, when the hot, dry wind called the *loo* blew into the city of

Karachi, he grabbed Saba's hand and tugged her down the four flights of stairs in their building, past orange, paan-stained corners and candy wrappers and sticky, black dirt, and out onto the pavement. He told her to look up and see the whiteness of the sky and the utter absence of clouds. Saba nodded in an absentminded way; she had left their dinner on the stove and didn't want it to burn.

She made an inventory in her head of everything that made her cringe: the cushions on the sofas, which had been flattened a long time ago, and the mattress on the bed, which had stains, which she avoided looking at when changing the two bedsheets she covered it with. The floor under her feet felt gritty, even after she swept and mopped it. It was always warm inside their apartment. The fans on the ceilings moved slowly, and when she asked Kamil about them, he said there was something wrong with the wiring, waving a hand vaguely, as if the answer lay somewhere over his right shoulder. It became hotter as the days went by, and when Saba cooked in the narrow kitchen, she felt fetidness rising in small waves from the dark space between the stove and the counter. Once, after an argument with Kamil, she cut her finger moving a piece of ginger against the jagged teeth of a grater. She put her hand in the bowl and squeezed out the blood and mixed the food with the specks of red. It was some comfort seeing him eat it distractedly, the way he ate almost every meal.

Each morning, she entered her office full of gratitude for the air-conditioning and went to the bathroom to gently wipe the sweat off her upper lip and to reapply her lipstick. On her soft chair behind the shiny counter, she sometimes felt bad about

Kamil. He was one of those who had to work outdoors and shiver in the quiet, raspy warmth of the wind. She imagined him going around the city on his motorcycle on assignments, sweating under the helmet, interviewing pedestrians and pro-testors, penciling down statistics in a small notebook which he held in his browned, veined hands. When he had to stay out past dinner Saba was happier because she didn't know how to speak to him for longer than five minutes. His conversation was in the format of opinions, and she assumed it was that way because he was always sending in articles to his newspaper. When he talked, he leaned forward as if to drive his points home with his spittle. If ever she had to identify his body she knew she would have to look for a mole under his left brow. She could not call him a bad husband, even after he once grabbed her arms in exasperation because she had refused to counter his opinion with one of her own. He let go of her with a jerk and called her "mild" as if it were a swear word.

———————

Kamil told Saba about a new assignment he had gotten from his editor: he had to write an article about the effect of heat on poor people. He looked determined and important, as if the weather were a criminal and he had to expose it. Sometimes he shared with Saba the results of his research, speaking pro-fessorially. He related incidents from his memory and from scrawls in his little notebook. He told her that in the slum areas the heat had solidified the air into a sulfurous yellow, and that a charity group had funded vans to be turned into ambulances, which stopped wherever they saw clumps of flies because almost always there was a body underneath. He swore and slapped the table for emphasis and, sometimes, he gritted his teeth when he spoke.

Once, after dinner, he threw a newspaper into her lap. "Read that," he said with a grimace, and paced the floor with the air of a person who had been grievously injured.

Saba dutifully read the sordid piece of news: in a narrow alley, an old man had been found wheezing. Rescuers discovered that he had been unable to ask for something to quench his thirst with because the sun had dried up all the water in his body, even his spit. Saba folded the newspaper and made sure that her face showed that she, too, had a heart for the dying downtrodden. In fact, she really thought that when there was no electricity the two of them could be good subjects for Kamil's research. She didn't say that out loud, though.

Over dinner, tearing his bread with angry flicks of his wrists, he complained about the city's lack of preparation for the heat wave and the idiocy of the population. He asked Saba if she felt it too, and for a moment she was puzzled—did he mean the heat or the idiocy? But, wisely, she just said yes. He hovered around her when she washed the dishes, not letting her use more than a trickle of water from the tap, telling her how three people had been found dead in a small, unpainted house, apparently strangled by the heat and the resulting thirst. He also reduced his bathing to once a week; he said more than that was a crime. That annoyed Saba. She had to lie next to him every night. Even with her back turned she could smell him. She had to wait for him to fall asleep before she went to the bathroom to clean herself, soaking a towel with water and wiping the soap off her body. Her hair was the hardest to clean because it was thick and curly. Sometimes it took her thirty minutes to get all the shampoo out. When their electricity started going out for eight hours at a time and opening the windows only brought in more suffocating air, Saba started testing her limits, and his: she shut doors and cupboards with angry bangs and let water gush out of taps at full strength. That drove Kamil wild and he pulled his hair and called her names.

One evening he stalked into the kitchen where she was washing a teaspoon and wrested it from her soapy hands. She shouted that he smelled like garbage and he hit her in the face. Right away, he looked horrified at what he had done. He stammered that he was terribly sorry, that it was the heat, or all those thirsty people clutching their throats as they died one by one by the sides of roads he went on every day. Saba stayed quiet, scrutinizing the event, like a scientist in a lab coat peering quizzically at an unidentified object. She did not feel angry at Kamil, and she recognized that was a curious thing. Instead, she imagined severing her nerve endings with tiny scissors, and shutting off her pores, sealing herself in. A little later, Kamil tried to show her that he loved her, or was committed to her, or to the idea of marriage, or something. She wasn't sure what. But she let him apologize to her, in their small, hot bedroom with no windows until, exhausted, he fell asleep.

Early the next morning, Saba woke up from the humidity. Her pillow was damp with sweat. She put her hands on her stomach and, through the thin cotton that covered it, knew that the division of her pale cells had begun. She made up her mind that she was not going to share this bit of clairvoyance with anyone, not even her husband, whose child was forming inside her. He lay on the other side of the bed, his shirt sticking to his front, and his face covered with stubble that seemed to grow in hours. Saba did not feel like reaching out and moving the hair from his forehead. Instead, she turned her thoughts inward, to the filling and emptying of her lungs, to the tiny lub-dub of her heart pulsing inside her wrist. She swung her legs off the bed and got dressed to go to work. There was gravity and deliberation in her movements, as if this secret child was filling her with grace. In the mirror, her face appeared to be unlined, pale and beautiful. She looked at the large, purpling bruise, found two bandages, and stuck them on her forehead.

———————

For the first few weeks, Saba's arms and face and fingers did not show signs of internal changes. In the lobby of her office building, behind the reception counter, she patted her stomach. When she wasn't answering calls and directing visitors, she whispered memos to the baby. She described to it the clothes on the women who stood in front of elevators to go to higher floors for more complicated jobs. If someone wore a more daring eyeshadow than was usual for her, Saba told the baby. She always spoke admiringly about these women. They had smooth foreheads, there didn't seem to be any bruises hidden there, though of course she couldn't tell unless she touched their faces. She balled up her fists to resist the urge to go up to them and find out, and let herself believe that these were complete women, beloved women.

"I think that blue suits her, oh, look at the print on the back," she would softly say to the baby.

Then the elevator doors would open and take them all away from her.

At home, she ignored Kamil and read to the baby—instructions from the backs of shampoo bottles, the list of side effects from packets of painkillers. She took care to eat her fruits, vegetables, and chicken. She wanted her child to be God-conscious, so she read to it from her Holy Book. Sometimes at work during breaks she read bits of news—not written by Kamil, but by others in other newspapers—about the rising temperature in the city. "Alarming! Record breaking!" the newspapers said. Such stories gave her perspective, she found. She read a paragraph about a young man, identified as Hamid, found face down on the mass of fat wires and gray pipes under the bonnet of his car. His face had to be unstuck from the machinery, and his mother had identified his body. It was too gruesome a story to read to her baby, so Saba folded the newspaper and hummed a tune to her stomach and finished an entire bottle of water. She started checking how much she was sweating and moved as little as possible when she stood outside after work to catch a rickshaw for home. To keep the baby cool, she thought about snow and ice cubes and refused to look at the sky. The bruise on her forehead faded slowly, though in certain lights she could trace its original outline.

One evening, Kamil held her chin in his fingers as if it were a grape, crushable and small, and turned her face toward his.

Then he let go and lightly said, "There's hardly a bruise there now." He sounded pleased, like he had when his favorite shoe was mended.

This was how they settled back into their normal routines, just like after other fights. Watching his mouth twist into shapes as he ranted, she mulled over the idea of telling him she was pregnant. Because she didn't want to completely shock him, she started off by relating her own anecdotes from work, like when her paycheck had gone to the wrong person because of a misspelling or a joke she'd heard at the water cooler. But Kamil puffed out his cheeks and let the air escape slowly as she spoke, and she realized that he did not have much patience for incidents that took place in air-conditioned interiors. So she withheld her big news from him. The baby inside her gave her the strength to apologize for her stories. Right away, Kamil forgave her. His voice flowed around her, blurring pleasantly, and she nodded and smiled, comforted that under her clothes, her secret was thriving and pushing out her skin. She spoke to the baby in her head, imagining the words going down her blood stream and into its umbilical cord.

In episodes, she told the baby all about how she and Kamil had gotten married. When she was twenty-six years old, her mother had become worried that her daughter was going to stay single forever. She took her to see a baba, a discreet old sage, who was known to have cures for problems like infertility, singlehood, cheating spouses, and divorce. His house was very far away, somewhere among the shanties but better than them. A small child let them in. Saba couldn't tell if the child was a boy or a girl; its hair was short and matted, and its eyes had been outlined with kohl. They followed its bare legs to a tree, under which sat the baba on a cushion. He asked Saba to lay her hand on the top of a small table, palm side up. He prodded it in a couple of spots and muttered, and once he rattled the fat yellow beads around his neck, and once he pulled his tangled gray beard, and, so caught up in the moment became Saba, that when thunder crackled above their heads, she believed she was cured. Two weeks later, Kamil and his mother visited her house. They had seen her picture, given to them by a matchmaking lady, and had liked her face. Kamil was twenty-eight and had nice manners and a decent job. Saba's mother raised her hands in speechless gratitude, and Saba and Kamil got married.

In preparation for the baby, Saba started scrubbing the apartment. The corners were the hardest because each one she confronted had a peeling table standing there, with an object on it that had stopped working, or piles of old telephone directories, or dust. She gazed critically at a lamp with a faded, blue shade and flipped through a directory to look up names for the baby, then swept everything into plastic bags. On a weekend, she stood back with her hands on her waist and surveyed the results. The heated light coming through the grimy, barred windows dimmed the effect of her hard work, but she was still pleased. She decided that one day she would paper that particular wall and that window. For some time at least, her child would be spared knowledge of the danger of agile intruders who could break into safe abodes, and the necessity of ugly bars. While she cleaned, Kamil worked in his corner of the living room, glancing at her with a frown every now and then.

"You're making too much noise."

Saba wondered if this was what companionship was.

Sometimes, when she saw him sitting over his papers and notes, feverishly writing away at his Very Important Piece, she wanted to tell him her secret. More specifically, she wanted to gloat at the look of shock on his face. Perhaps he would be so astounded that he had undermined her that he would sink to his knees and hit the floor with his forehead.

There was no doubt in her mind that the baby was growing fine, even though her stomach only looked flabby, not taut, when she stood sideways in front of the mirror. She tried to glean knowledge of the baby's gender, but her sensitive fingers only told her that the naughty baby had crossed its legs, or curled up tight, refusing to let its mother know. She made plans for educating the child, after which he or she would grow up to earn some money, and the two of them would live in a nice little place by themselves. She imagined Kamil calling to ask if he could visit, and she and her grown child looking at each other and laughing at the very idea.

———

Kamil said his editor was getting worried about the article being printed in time. There had been news from the meteorological station about rain in the next few weeks. Also, Kamil said, squeezing his forehead, the imams of the city's mosques had started to pray for rain every Friday after afternoon prayers.

A lot of times he came home then went out again, returning for a few hours between midnight and dawn.

"Wrapping up a few details," he said to the notebook in front of him, even though Saba hadn't asked him.

She had decided she was not going to be curious about his movements. She chose, instead, to feel irritated. She told herself that it was getting harder for her to rest now because her back ached. She discovered that the trick to falling asleep was to not start listening for the sounds of her husband closing the front door and his motorcycle rumbling down the street and the moon coming up and the moon going down and the motorcycle rumbling to a stop and the other side of the bed creaking.

———————

Kamil's article was published, and one week later, clouds crowded around and everyone in the city held their breath, and then it rained. Kamil, who had started to look like a dehydrated stick with glittering black eyes, turned shiny with the muggy air and with the congratulations he received on his fine work. He brought home samosas and held out a copy of the newspaper in front of Saba—he didn't let her touch it because her hands were greasy from the food.

"It's a feature piece," he said proudly. "My best work, the editor says. I might even get an award for it, though he has asked me not to mention that in front of anybody yet."

Saba made herself smile. She felt an urge to touch her forehead again and wince, but she wasn't sure she could handle what would follow. What if Kamil got angry? What if he laughed about it? What if he didn't remember what he had done? And her old bruise didn't hurt anymore, anyway. It hadn't hurt for a long time, and so what if Kamil was going to receive an award for some humanitarian words? She held inside her far more than he was ever going to get to hold in his thick fingers.

For about nine days, it rained almost nonstop. Roads flooded but people crossed them joyously, hitching up shalwar and pants. Umbrellas were optional. Schools closed for a whole day to celebrate the end of the worst heat wave in forty years. Some of the poorer people died because of electrocution. Kamil wrote a small piece on how they should have known better than to bathe in puddles where wires had fallen. He showed it to Saba, and, late at night, she used those pages to scrub the toilet.

His minor success seemed to have made him generous toward her. He asked her one night about her work, but she didn't have any interesting details to relate. She told him that they had switched from blue sticky notes to green ones.

She was surprised when he came home one evening with a new handbag for her.

"You never get anything for yourself," he said, gentle admonition in his voice.

She hung the bag from her mirror. She knew where it was from. It had swung from the post of the cart of the man who sold fake bags and shoes at the corner of their street. When she lay in bed, she saw its bright, golden clasp gleaming cheaply in the dim light. It reminded her that the building she lived in was old and a sickly shade of yellow, that most of the year the trees and shrubs outside hung dispirited and dusty, growing out of cracks in footpaths, and that no amount of rain could give them beauty. Maybe she and Kamil had never had a chance because of the street they lived on—narrow, dirty, trapping the heat that poured from the sky in the day, releasing it in waves from the melting asphalt in the night. Even rainwater couldn't flow down it gracefully: already there were plastic bags and pieces of food from vendors' carts mixed in it.

She had seen handbags like that when she was small, in apartments like this one on streets like hers. Always, the women holding them wore bright maroon lipstick and clutched their men around the waist on motorcycles, or walked fast through marketplaces holding the hands of little children who wore shirts with words on them like "sweet girl" or "cool guy." Her mother had been one of them herself, had had friends like these, and Saba used to visit them with her, wearing an ironed frock. When the women talked about their husbands, who were tailors or butchers or electricians, they used pronouns because Saba was sitting with them. She understood anyway, listening to every word while pretending to be absorbed in eating the biscuits. The topics hardly ever changed: their men's tempers, excesses, and taciturn ways.

Like everyone else, though, Saba had been sure she was going to have it different, and better.

The rain stopped. Kamil told Saba that he wanted to drop her off at work. He wouldn't listen when she said that she could go on her own, so she agreed and got onto the motorcycle behind him. It was necessary that she put an arm around him, to have something to hold on to. They bumped along, and Saba sent reassuring messages to the baby in case the new sensations were worrying it. Puddles lay on the road like trick rugs. Kamil went around them whenever he could, a detail which Saba would remember later, and which would make her think that he was a kind man. He was going slowly through a spot of shallow water when a van spun toward them. It roared, or screamed, Saba wasn't sure. For some brief, wonderful seconds, she and Kamil flew through moisture and air. When she opened her eyes, she was on the road, as if lying on the bed with Kamil, the gray of the sky above them. She pressed her stomach for company, but the baby didn't talk to her, and she worried if it was upset at something she had said, or done, or eaten. There was a lump-like hardness inside her. She waited to understand if the pain she was feeling was real or imaginary, and she decided that it was very real, not unlike the kind she used to get before and during her period, which of course hadn't happened for a long time because her baby had been real, just like this pain. When it subsided, the leaden weight inside her settled like sediment and filled her with a new kind of gravity, unlike the one she had experienced that morning when the baby was a dot.

And so, she did not feel sad about the loss of her child. The appropriate amount of grief will come later, she comforted herself. Her head and belly felt sodden and she longed to get away from the mess. Vaguely, she wondered if Kamil, too, wanted to go away. She couldn't turn her neck to see how he was doing. If only he had a pillow under his head, she thought. Did this concern of hers mean that she loved him? If she could move her hand, she'd have clutched her chest. What if the van hadn't hit them? She would have missed out on loving her man. The close-call nature of it all filled her with exhilaration and delicious sorrow. Lying in the puddle, she squared her shoulders and decided that if she hadn't taken care of Kamil before, she would do so now. A twinge of regret made its way to her mind at all the times she could have wiped Kamil's brow, or brought him a glass of water, or checked his work for mistakes, but hadn't. But you couldn't hurry things, she told herself. They happened only when all necessary conditions had been fulfilled. After all, each event existed merely as a result of a previous one. Before this love was the event of the baby, and before that was her marriage to Kamil, and the old baba she'd met with her mother, and her own parents' existence. So really, it was almost impossible to tell what or who to blame or thank. She moved her hand until she found Kamil's cold, still one, wrinkled with water, and she held on to it like a burr and waited for someone to find them.

TOGETHER

THE YEAR WE MET for the second time was when Sara had her second baby and I had my first. She'd said to the others, I found out later, to bring gifts for my baby. They brought gifts for Sara's child, too, because they were sweet women. "We weren't going to forget about you!" they laughed. And Sara made that funny sound: *pfft*—with the "Come on! My baby's not news!" look. It was such a warm look and made us feel like we had every right to be in her big house, served by her maid, her cook, her chauffeur, and her gardener.

Amal asked how things were between me and my husband, and I laughed and rolled my eyes and said, "Oh you know. Work work work. I might as well be invisible." This was not true. When the baby was born, my husband put aside his projects—documentaries he wanted to make—to spend more time at home. He even brought me flowers sometimes. When I nursed the baby, he stroked my flabby arm and said we were such a lucky little family to not care about money. As soon as the baby was done, I handed her to him and ran to the bathroom and pretended to take a shower. One afternoon I was in there with the water on when I found my tweezers and an old, bad habit. I found that cutting still felt good, even with a pair of blunt ends.

I made the mistake of telling this to Sara. She said I had the "baby blues," and that I was lucky to have such a devoted husband, not like poor Amal—she never knew when hers was coming or going. A few days later, I called Sara and told her I was much better now; she had been such a help.

In Sara's home, in a corner, Amal pressed a small box tied with a ribbon into my hands and whispered that she was so happy for me. At the door as we were leaving Mina warned me about eating too much—babies sucked energy and life out of a woman, leaving an enormous vacuum inside the mother's body. Her mother had told her this. All of my friends helped me carry the gifts to my car.

The next year, my husband made a short film about water and won a small award. He had worked hard on his film. He'd skipped meals, become hollow-cheeked, let his hair go uncombed for days. I'd shake him awake as he lay on the couch in last week's clothes and bring him trays of warmed meals. Once, at midnight, his eyes bright with caffeine, he asked me, "Do you see how water is everywhere? *Everywhere.*" He jabbed the air with his long fingers.

Sometimes, when I walked the baby to sleep, I could hear water sloshing in my cells.

Amal called to congratulate us about the award as if it were a family achievement. If there was one thing I could not stand, it was people who pretended to be happy for you when really all they wanted was for you to be hit by a bus. Sara called as well, but it was to say that we must meet again, all of us with our children so they could love one another the way we did. We were like sisters to her, her soul friends! She wanted to make food for us. Please, could we please meet? She had new covers on the sofas, and there were two lamps with hand-painted shades, and she would be devastated if we refused to go see her.

I did not want to go to Sara's house. I did not want to see anybody. The baby was growing, growing, and becoming louder, and there was always something to do in each room of our apartment. I was always hungry and dry-skinned and smelly.

We ended up visiting Amal. "I need some good, solid advice because things are a little tricky around here," she said on the phone, speaking clearly and calmly. Her words, if written down, would look like planes taking off. I went with my daughter to her house. She lived closer to the south of the city and had tried to be tasteful about how she decorated her home. I have never forgotten the hideous red and orange rug she nailed to the wall in her drawing room.

Mina had let her hair grow absurdly long, all the way down to her waist. It made her look shorter and childish, but what we said was that she looked younger. She played with our children while Amal told us that if her husband didn't care about his wife and his child, then she had no use for him. Did we think she should get a divorce? Her voice was as strong as wood.

Sara said, "No! You need a marriage counselor."

Mina said, "Maybe you should stay together for your daughter."

I said, "You will be so lonely, Amal."

Then Amal cried long and hard. I had never seen her do that—not when we were little and she'd fallen into wet mud and all the children laughed at her, not in college when a boy she liked told her she bored him. Amal, beautiful Amal, who always chased and chased. In school, she trained the insides of our chests to get worked up into a fevered state, oscillating between agony and ecstasy. She used to push herself away from the school wall and me and walk toward the crowd of loosened ties and tanned arms. I stayed back, imagined her heart beating with the inevitability of her attractiveness. And now here she was.

Later that day, she made us tea and we felt better. We looked at our little ones playing next to one another and smiled and fed them cake.

And later, the next year, my husband became thinner and cried sometimes and bought me a flower one evening to apologize for all the sadness in his heart. He wiped his nose and his eyes, shut his notebook of crossed out ideas, and said in a voice full of resolve, "I'm not going to sit around and wait to be appreciated by ingrates. Thank you for standing by me." When he won another little award, his voice became stronger and happier. This time, the documentary had been about food, perhaps because he'd been consuming so little of it for fear of wasting it.

We used some of the prize money for a holiday in another city. Our children played in the swimming pool and collected shells on the beach. My husband wrote and wrote in his notebook. Whenever he looked up to smile at the children, the sun in his eyes made him look golden. The sea looked so beautiful that I had to imagine a conversation. *"What are those lines?" he asked, his eyes on my forearm, his face crowded with concern and surprise. "Stretch marks," I said, radiant with his attention.*

That was a good time in our lives.

Once, we went to a small dinner party. The host had a broad, kind smile and wrinkled clothes. He was shorter than me and I felt bad that I had to look down on him, especially since I knew he wasn't having any luck being a writer.

My husband was full of talk on the way back. The woman in the hideous orange dress, who'd sat next to me, was an artist, but after ten years had yet to sell a painting. She held exhibitions in galleries because her father left her a lot of money and her husband was a wealthy cardiologist. The man with the mustache was a writer. He wrangled publication in third-tier journals. He had no wife; he thought being married would distort him. The inseparable couple had ordinary jobs—she was a teacher and he worked in a bank. They made up for that by traveling to two extraordinary destinations every year. Or maybe they went to ordinary places in unusual ways.

"Imagine being together for weeks like that," my husband said. "We're lucky, aren't we, having our own things to do."

An image came to mind: me, running a vacuum cleaner across a carpet, then lifting the nozzle to catch an escaped feather. The nozzle and my triumphant smile were bright in the sunlight. It was too bad no one was home to witness the brilliancy of that moment.

Another good thing happened that year: Mina and her husband moved to a house on the same street as Sara. I couldn't help thinking about them often: *Now they must be having tea. Now they must be talking, heads bent close.*

One afternoon some years later, Mina called to tell me she'd seen Sara's son riding his bicycle, talking loudly and shaking his fist at no one she could see. Mina's breath was tight with excitement. "What should we do?" we'd wondered. In the end, we thought it best to keep it to ourselves. We didn't want to embarrass our dear friend.

I felt a little closer to Mina after this. Still, the thought of her standing in her kitchen, thin arms making meals for her family, irritated me a little.

Soon after, Sara called asking for help. She said she had no one to turn to, and I said that was nonsense—what were old friends for? By the time I finished the laundry and the cooking and the ironing and finally went to see Sara—it had taken a few days, maybe—her son was already in the psych ward of a government hospital.

"He should be in a better place," Sara said, shrinking into the thin waiting room chair, not looking at the people who walked about with black holes for eyes, the people who muttered.

"You can always sell your chandeliers," I suggested. She turned away. People we didn't know gave her son medicines and shots and goodness knows what else behind a door at the end of the corridor. Somebody was crying in a room but thank God it wasn't the one with her son. I felt special; Sara had called me and no one else, and I worried about how I could surpass her expectations. I bought her a cup of tea and a packet of biscuits and a small, thick magazine.

Sara's son used to go to the same school as my daughter.

She never mentioned him, not even when he stopped going to school. Sometimes I worried that maybe someone else wouldn't talk about my children either, and I would miss the warning signs. I started asking them more questions about their friends and their fears, and I tried to listen for longer. I used concealer under my eyes and perfume on my clothes so they wouldn't notice the burdens their father wore on his face. He had not won an award in a long time.

Later, when all our children were done with school, we went to Sara's. This was because we felt sorry for her. Our children were moving on to universities and jobs, and her son was in the hospital again. She leaned against her dining table. She looked like a bunch of splintering sticks held together at the neck. In school, all the girls had wanted her thinness, she'd told us once.

She saw our faces and smiled. "Talk, please! Let me hear your lovely voices. I have missed you, you know."

Mina, narrow, hard, and slightly sour, said to Amal, "Tell your daughter to get married."

"Why would she want to get married? Look at me!" Amal laughed at herself for a few seconds and when she stopped, the corners of her mouth were lower than before. I did not feel sorry for her because she looked so strong, so healthy, so beautiful. She looked like she could travel alone over the continents and sail their rivers, giving her independent daughter a pat on the back along the way.

"It is ungratefulness, is what it is," Mina said to no one in particular. She spoke about our children, for lack of her own, as if they were hers too. When she criticized them, we tried to stamp hard on our egos.

"Well. Three out of five isn't bad," Amal said, also speaking in the possessive about all of our children, the entire collection.

"Go visit your daughter, Sara," Mina said.

Amal had once said Sara worried that if she visited her daughter it would turn her luck upside down. It would make her husband leave her; it would make her children crippled.

That's why she only spoke to her on the phone and tickled her grandkids long-distance.

I tried to recall the face of Sara's daughter. She had gotten married and moved to a house in the suburbs in faraway Canada. I could only remember a school photograph. My children standing next to Amal's daughter and Sara's boy and girl. They were in their school uniforms, squinting in the morning sun. Our children had shrieked one another's names while playing in the rooms and lawns of our homes. Sometimes we had allowed ourselves to relax a little and really sit back. Sometimes we'd even managed to detach the ghosts of our past failures and future hopes from them.

I wanted to go home now, but it wasn't time to leave yet and they would have asked me too many solicitous questions. What I did instead was stop looking at the faces of my friends. I tried to look interested in my surroundings. The two chandeliers in Sara's drawing room, heavy and rhombus-shaped, looked dusty. There were age spots in the mirror with the ornate frame.

Sara brought out food. She had cooked so much. There were pots full of rice and chicken and fried fish and soup and beef.

"I take him meals every day in the hospital," she said. "I label his boxes so they know it's his and no one else's." She turned to me. "How is your son?"

"Oh, you know," I said, swatting the air as if my son made me mad. "He's too busy for his old mother. Like father, like son." That did not seem enough, so I talked about how, on her wedding day, my daughter had gouged small holes in her nail polish and picked the skin around her nails until she bled.

Amal looked at Sara and issued statements like a seer. "Your son, you'll see, he will get out of that psych ward, and he will be perfectly fine. It's just a matter of time. He will have a good job, and he will get married. And you'll end up with a daughter-in-law, just like on TV, and you'll wonder what the fuss was all about."

I thought, almost idly, *Maybe she could pay the girl to bear her son's rages.*

In the beginning, we were full of solutions. We used to know all about how to correct marriages going off course, how to fix the anxieties of our growing children. *If she would only,* we used to think. Here we were now, so altered that our past selves would not have recognized us.

When I got back home, I pulled down the sheet that I had draped over the mirror in my bedroom. *I am still here,* I thought with some surprise. Then I went to the kitchen to put away the food Sara had sent us all home with. It was one of the ways she liked to take care of us.

PRESENT TENSE

WHAT I REMEMBER MOST from when I was a child is a time when my father did not come home one day, and not the next day, or the day after. I was twelve and my brother was fifteen. The first few days of his absence I woke up in a state of anxiety, my body filling up with the unpleasantness of this great uncertainty my brother, my mother and I were thrust into. I felt better among the wooden, lidded desks in my classroom and the faces of my teachers, and by afternoon recess, I was at the peak of my day's happiness. In the evening, as six o'clock came nearer—the time my father usually came home—I was paralyzed with worry and sat in the corner of the living room, only able to move again when the hour hand came to rest on the seven. After a strange meal with my shrunken family, I would sink into sleep, grateful that my father was still gone, and uncomfortable with myself for feeling this way.

I wanted to be assured of his staying away longer but didn't know how to talk to my mother about it. Besides, my brother was already doing the asking. She gave him a different answer each time. "He is visiting relatives," or, "He needs to be at work," or, "He comes home late and goes to work before you wake up." One evening, she was humming and sorting out a pile of old books and I guess that made my brother wonder if she had killed our father. His face turned red and he shouted at her and called her selfish. She paused in her task and said, sharp as a chip of ice, "Your father is perfectly fine." She always called him "your father" when she was angry and wanted to hold us, his sons, responsible for his presence, as if our births had made him a necessary evil in her life. And when she said those two words now, I felt twisted with sadness because I'd thought that with him gone, she would like her sons better. My brother stomped away but I stood a while longer, watching her face anxiously. I felt lighter only when she started to hum again.

———————

My father has come to the airport to pick me up. I feel jittery and uncertain, reduced from my adult height to a child's dimensions. But I keep control of my suitcase and make sure he sees me tipping a porter, even though we haven't taken his help, and by the time we walk to the car I am a grownup again. I have not been in Karachi for seven years; I have not sat next to my father for just as long. He is old now, and his fingers, curved over the steering wheel, are thin. He peers through the windshield and drives in bursts of speed, dodging motorcycles and rickshaws. His window is rolled down and he instructs me to do the same.

"Cross ventilation," he says over the noise of a bus horn.

I say, "We should get the air-conditioner fixed."

"There's no need to throw away good money," he says. "You don't understand."

I pull out my cell phone and swipe the screen, even though there isn't anyone I need to assure that I have arrived safely.

"Put that away," my father says. "Put it under you. Don't you read the news?"

I wonder why I have chosen to be here again. A lump grows in my stomach the closer we get to the house I grew up in. I struggle to stay in the future, thinking about the day I would return to the airport and fly across comforting barriers of mountains and oceans to my other continent, to my other city where problems come in neat packages no bigger than the palm of my hand. When that fails, I try to ground myself in the very seconds of the present—the feel of the thin seat cover, the roughness of my nails. Sometimes a new underpass or a flyover or a shiny mall distracts me and that is good, but then I see a piece of wall I often passed when I was little and I am again pulled thinly, painfully, through that narrow corridor between the past and the future, between that which we can never change and that which gives us a chance to escape.

———————

My brother blamed our mother. He watched her through narrowed eyes.

"She knows where he is. She is lying to us," he said to me at least twice a day.

If we were in the school van and I was laughing at something a friend said, he would pinch me and hiss those words into my ear. I would immediately turn away from the joke and remove the grin from my face.

"Do you miss him? Our father?" he would ask me in a tight voice.

I would lie and say, "Yes. Of course I do."

Secretly, I would relish the feel of slackness in my limbs and my insides, the ability of my lungs to balloon to full capacity.

We had grown up on thin air, the oxygen sucked up by our father and mother's moods. We were curved and wiry and tense like antennae, picking up signals of impending storms from the way our father snapped his newspaper or how our mother shut the fridge door. Too sharp a sound meant that, soon, old wounds were going to be reopened with blade-like words. Sometimes I mouthed along, being my father and mother by turns like an actor playing two roles. Other times I went to my brother and found him elaborately coloring in a map, or a picture of the human heart, or an eyeball, or the circulation system.

He wanted me to have a good opinion of our father. He said that a long time ago, before we were born, our father had gone without a lot of things so he could save money for his future children. He had eaten only one solid meal a day, did not have chicken more than once a month, and walked to most places under the blazing sun. Then, when he had enough money, he got this whole house built, just for us. He put three bedrooms in it, each a different color—yellow, green, and blue. The boundary wall surrounding the house was also an example of how much he cared—it had shards of glass set on the top to stop burglars from climbing over and robbing him of his possessions.

From the other room, we heard a roar.

My brother said, "You can see why he's like that, right? It's because of *her*. He can't help it."

———————

My mother has given me the firmest mattress in the house and put a brand-new bedsheet over it. There is no comforter, only a second sheet. It is too warm for anything thicker. I am in my old room, of course. In some places, the yellow paint has started flaking off the wall in irregular shapes, and I have the urge to peel them. I count three brown arches of water stains in the corners. The bathroom mirror is speckled and my face appears gray.

"Do you need more money?" I ask my mother. I am unable to meet her eyes, guilty that I have not been here until now, guilty that I want to leave.

"We are comfortable, son," she says.

She makes me two rotis and watches me eat. She complains about my brother. I ask her to give him a call and she says, "He is happy in his own life. He has no regard for us."

I speak to him that night. He lives on another continent, a third one. He has not visited Karachi in close to ten years. I tell him the house looks small and helpless, that things aren't what they used to be; they are peaceful. He tells me he is done talking and hands the phone to his wife. I tell her my brother ought to come see his aging parents, and she explains to me that his doctor—his therapist—says he is prone to melancholia and being back there would make him morose, which is bad for their children who are precious and innocent.

My brother still thinks that our father—and maybe our mother—owes us an explanation and an apology.

———

Whenever they fought it was my mother who looked crazy. Her hair came out of her bun, her breath expelled itself loudly through her nostrils and teeth, her fists bunched up. She had a way of moaning and clutching her clothes. Once I watched, terrified and fascinated, as she picked up a slipper and slapped her own thighs with it. She liked to grab my arm and say to my father, in a tearful, triumphant way, "I have my children. I have *my* children." That always made me feel happy and strong, and I glowered at my father. I promised myself that if he offered to drive me to school I would say no.

When he wasn't roaring, he was unremarkable in shape and size. He was thin and walked with a slight slouch, which made him appear genial. His eyes, when amused, were mild. He liked to tell me and my brother we had a lot to learn and took us with him on errands. He spoke kindly to petrol station attendants and mechanics, and if their skin was the same dark brown as his, he gave them a tip and told them a joke.

"These are our brothers, hard-working immigrants from India," he would say to us. "Look how they sweat for their bread."

He spoke as if he were correcting a fault in us.

We would pass a plot of land where light-skinned men, burned red from the sun, carried bricks and disappeared behind new walls of other people's houses. Sometimes one of them would look up and his eyes would flash green or blue. Our father would point to the men and say, "Watch out for these lazy, dirty people, come down from the north to cause us trouble, setting up shacks. You know that bomb that went off in Lyari? Them. That riot in Saddar? Them."

I worried that these men looked like my mother; her light brown eyes could appear green. Once I asked her where she was from, and she laughed and said, "Here. I was born right here in Karachi."

My brother tells me that he wants to come see our parents. His voice is robust, and he says his therapist thinks he is ready. He says he will look into his schedule and flights. He might even bring the wife and children.

I take my father to an eye doctor to get him a pair of glasses. He goes through the tests with grim resignation. Back in the car he says, "That was an Urdu-speaking doctor, which is why I let him check me." A little later, he points to a string of shops. "New business going up everywhere. Karachi is still the City of Lights." And he looks at me as if I have challenged him.

For many evenings, my brother waited by the window for our father, sitting on a chair with his knees drawn up to his chin. He stopped playing with his friends. One day, on our way home from school, we saw a bus on fire. As our driver pressed hard on the brake and turned around the school van, my friends and I leaned out and saw flames leaping out of the bus's windows like so many strange passengers. There were some men around it, yelling and laughing.

One of them drew back his arm and, with the grace of a javelin thrower at the Olympics, hurled his lit-up torch at the bus. The driver shouted at us to get away from the windows, to shut them. The men might attack us next. My brother drew his head in reluctantly.

He started buying newspapers from the shop at the corner and looked through them all, reading out loud reports of kidnappings of activists, of their bodies found in trash heaps.

"Our father is one of them. He's been taken away," he said.

I imagined our father in the back of a black car with tinted windows, a man with a long mustache next to him with a rifle on his lap. My brother said I was to help him read the papers. If I said I was bored, he pounded the floor with his fist and said I was turning into our mother. So I'd bend my head again and peel skin off my heels and toes while names rolled by in front of my eyes like a monotonous landscape sketched in black ink.

He made me go around the house at night after our mother was asleep. He said he was looking for clues that might point to our father. He wanted to find out if our mother was one of the enemy agents, so we went into the kitchen and twisted open jars of spices and sniffed the contents to check for suspicious substances. We discovered that entering our parents' room was as easy as pushing their door open. We went there only one time, though. Our mother was alone, frowning in her sleep. My brother motioned for me to look under her bed, and I wondered what he would say if I found a gun there with our father's initials scratched into the barrel or a letter that apologized to our mother. But there was nothing except a pair of our father's slippers. I gave them to my brother and he held them to his chest.

Some nights he soundlessly turned the key in the front door and we went out to the lawn. The grass felt soothing to the tender, raw bottoms of my feet. I would stand with my brother in the dark until the sky began to lighten. Then we would go in to change for school.

One afternoon he forbade me from playing with the others and made me stand next to him right outside our gate.

"We have to meet someone," he said.

I thought he had made a new friend, and I felt sorry for him when the sun began to go down and still no one came. I watched other fathers arrive home, their cars pulling tiredly down the street and grinding up short slopes and through the gates of their houses. I imagined the men climbing out slowly in crumpled shirts and pants, collars unstarched from the day's work, smelling of cigarettes and exhaust fumes, like ours used to. I wondered what my father was doing, but I wondered about him as I would about people in an airplane passing overhead. We turned around and went back home, walking by our father's dusty car in the garage. On the weekend, my brother washed it and made it shine. He said it made our father feel closer to him.

My brother has curled up on his bed and not gone to work for three days now, his wife tells me. She sent their two children to her mother's until he feels better, and has asked his therapist to come over. My sister-in-law is a competent woman, not given to hysteria. She probably washed a set of dishes and ran the washing machine while she spoke to the doctor. I ask her if I ought to come over and she says that will not do anyone any good.

There has been no electricity in the house all morning. My father is reading a newspaper, taking off his glasses every few minutes to rub the bridge of his nose. My mother is asleep on the sofa, her face shiny. I think about things they both need. Handrails in the bathrooms? A generator, a driver, a full-time maid? A new house, a different continent? Not mine or my brother's but another of their very own, so that we all have space and live in happiness?

I doze off and wake to the sound of my father talking. My stomach contracts. But he is only telling my mother to go sit by the open window because there is a good breeze coming through; he says he will sleep somewhere else.

While my father was gone, my mother became beautiful. She grew thin and her skin became so pale it was almost transparent. When she stood under a strong light I could see little blue veins. She wore perfume and she held our books daintily so as not to ruin her polished fingernails. After my brother poured her bottle of nail color down the sink, she kept her nails bare again. One evening he slapped down a newspaper in front of her and told her to check it for our father's name among victims of recent incidents. And she did run her fingertip down the lists and articles detailing riots and mobs, but I felt she wasn't really reading, she was thinking about getting her hair done at the salon.

If she thought about our father or missed him, she didn't say so. She didn't mention him at all. In the morning she waited with us for the school van and told us we were not to step outside until the last bell rang and that we were to come straight home. She shook her head and wished we didn't have to go so far away; trouble could start anywhere in the city at any time. She moved toward my brother, but he stepped away from her reach. She busied herself with straightening my tie. She put her hands on my shoulders and said, "People are disappearing."

I was buoyed by her concern and did well on all my tests. In the mirror, I practiced smiles of gratitude I could give her. When she sat at the table with us she leaned over, her back a soft letter C, and this new pliancy made me unable to speak sometimes.

When our father was around, she would come out of the kitchen with a big knife in her hand and slam it on the table. Then she would flip through our schoolwork and if one of us got a sum wrong or had written untidily, she would throw the book at the wall or run a sharpened pencil down the page. Under the table I would pick the skin around my nails into tiny pieces, eyeing the blade, because I was sure that one day my mother would run it through us. All of us.

A woman came to visit her one evening. She brushed our hair off our foreheads and clicked her tongue and looked at us as if we had suddenly become fatherless boys, irreversibly so. She told us to take her little girl out to the lawn while the grownups talked. We sat on the grass and pulled up a few blades.

The girl asked, "Where is your father?"

My brother frowned and said, "He has gone for work."

"I heard our cleaning woman say he's left his wife and his children," she said.

My brother lunged toward her, grabbed her hair in his fist, and said, "Shut up."

I want to take my parents out to eat.

I do not want to take them anywhere, but that is what a good son does—fix his parents' health, fix their home, spoil them, because one spent her body in giving birth and the other worked at a job he did not like; because they stayed together for their children's sake; because they endured enormous pain believing they were doing us good.

My mother wants Chinese food. My father wants to know why I like to waste my money. In the car he puts a small cushion behind my mother's back and asks her how low does she want her window rolled down. They are extremely cheerful on the way to the restaurant. They point out all the work being done in the city.

"Look at that excavator," my father says.

"I don't see any piles of garbage here anymore," my mother says. "Tell me if you see any garbage."

"You should come back and settle down here, son," my father says. "Get married."

The present is slipping away from me again and I rub my fingers hard over the worn-out rubber on the steering wheel. Five thin scratches on the windshield, black dashboard, a truck visible in the side mirror.

I am thinking of how our father used to take us out sometimes on Thursdays, the last day of the work week. We wore shirts with collars and full pants, and our mother brushed our hair until it lay flat across our heads. She got dressed in soft colors and let her braid hang down her back instead of keeping it coiled viciously in a bun. She and my father parried gently-teasing words in low murmurs, his voice smooth and sure and content, hers full of secrets her children couldn't guess. I did not know how to participate in this sort of behavior, this display of affection. Maybe I had imagined seeing them spit at each other. I felt unsettled and even a little happy, the way an unpopular, blindfolded child in a game feels.

*   *   *

Around nine one night, after our mother had gone to sleep, my brother sat on the edge of my bed and said that we had something important to do. He had shadows under his eyes, I remember, and his face looked small and square. I followed him through doors and over the grass and when he started undoing the bolts of the gate I felt a spasm of fear in case our father had been hiding outside every night and was going to leap back in now, full of anger that we had kept him locked out. But there was nobody there, not even a beggar. There was a curfew in the city and everything shut at eight, long ago. I wanted to whisper, "Where are we going?" but my brother was taking long strides and the words stayed inside me and I went with him. Anxiety was a swarm of mosquitoes eating me alive. We reached the end of the street and I saw someone squatting on the dirt next to the trunk of an acacia tree. The figure stood up when we stopped and I could only tell that it was a man, and I remember how he smelled—of roses.

My brother held up an envelope. "Where is my father?" he said.

"Hand over the money first," the man said, muffled behind his scarf.

"First the information, son of a pig."

I remember my brother's voice, steadied by rage. I remember the man's white hand, the color my father preferred not to shake, grabbing the envelope and my brother trying to twist it out of his grasp. I remember his small gray silhouette dwarfed by the man's large one. I remember the man sinking a blade into my brother's leg and then running away. He crumpled onto the gravel and I was worried that he wouldn't be comfortable there.

I do not remember the walk back home or waking up my mother.

She said we needed to take my brother to a hospital. I sat next to him, holding a shirt over the wound on his thigh, the blood spreading up, away from gravity, onto my fingers. My mother started the engine, and I had a sudden picture of me and my brother, very small and still, watching from that same place in the back as our mother sat in the driver's seat, pale and pinched as a starved moon, gripping the steering wheel with bloodless hands, listening to our father tell her she was too dumb to learn to drive. We watched him grab the wheel and weave the car wildly to the left and right. But that night she drove, grimly and slowly, the sodium yellow of the streetlights making the closed shop shutters look uncompromising. On a side street, she stopped in front of a small house with a crescent and a star painted on its wall. Inside the poorly lit examination room there was a doctor, and he checked the injured leg. The sound of my brother's moans brought out small children from other parts of the doctor's house and they ran around the room barefoot, shrieking with happiness.

One day we came home from school to find our father on the sofa, wearing formal clothes as if he had come home from work early on a whim. He got up when he saw us and tried to pat our backs, but he couldn't because we had our school bags on. He let his arm fall to the side. There was no mark on his face, no fracture in his leg. He looked unbroken and clean shaven. There was a small suitcase by his feet, the kind people take with them when they deliberately choose to leave. "I'll leave the black socks and keep the brown ones," he might have said. "I'll leave the children and keep the distance." Perhaps my mother had helped him pack.

"Have you been good children?" he asked us.

He pulled a leather jacket from the suitcase and told my brother it was for him. I remember the smell of it—sharp and old. My brother put it on and stood there self-consciously, the jacket hanging over his skinny frame, his Adam's apple bobbing up and down nervously, his face flushed. My father gave me a shirt wrapped in cellophane. It was blue and had a collar. I took it and didn't say anything.

I could feel my brother shaking next to me and I wondered, as if from far away, if he also understood that our father had never really become one of the missing ones of the city, those written about in newspapers and lauded for martyrdom. Our mother brought out cups of tea for all of us, and our father turned on the news.

———————

"Are you having a good time? Is Mother spoiling you? Does she remember she has two sons?" asks my brother.

I think, *That is the work of his medication.* I have learned by now to bring out the correct expression and body language when he is at this stage of recovery.

"I'd forgotten how hot summer can be here," I say, raising my eyebrows and gesturing with my free hand as if I am on stage.

There is a pause, maybe a minute long, maybe two.

"I can't go there just yet," my brother says. "I looked, you know, and there's just no time, no time at all. The children's school, all this work. You should have planned this better. I would have come along. Maybe June. Would you be there in June? Would you stay there for me?"

TRANSACTIONS

FIRST, PATRICK HAS A bad reaction to the fish, and he is holding his stomach and moaning very softly, not drinking the fizzy ginger water I am holding in a glass. Then Mrs. Farzana from upstairs calls me and does not say, "How is your husband? How can I help you?" but only asks if I could give her daughter Nida an extra half an hour of chemistry class on Saturday because she failed her last test. I listen to her with one ear; she goes on about how Nida will drive her to her grave with her bad attitude, and I say some rubbish that no, no, she is a very bright child. Patrick squeezes his eyes shut and puts his head on his knees and I hiss to him, "Drink this!"

Mrs. Farzana says, "Being busy with extra classes will keep her away from her bad friends, and all this boyfriend-girlfriend nonsense. I cannot allow this in my house."

"I will be happy to help her," I say, then I wait for her to tell me she will pay me for the extra time, and for all the other hours I have spent teaching her useless child.

"I will send Nida tomorrow at ten in the morning." Mrs. Farzana shuts the phone in my ear and I am left holding the receiver like a dummy. I am angry but I do not have time to stay that way because Patrick is now stumbling toward the bathroom.

I let him watch three hours of TV that evening. It is the only way he agrees to drink water of aniseeds and fennel, and afterward take in a light tea with dry toast. He is fussy and tiresome when the nine o'clock news finishes and it is time to go to bed. He says, "You never leave any soda for me." And, "Tomorrow you will make me halwa. Always you are too busy, busy, busy."

I am the best secondary school chemistry tutor in Karachi. I write on the board, "Anise has anethol and fennel is a carminative." My students ask, "Is this going to be in our exams?" I tell them no, and they put down their pens. I write, "Pimpinella anisum" and "Foeniculum vulgare" and they giggle.

I have taught for more than forty years, and I never used to teach on public holidays or weekends. I never taught on Christmas or Easter. But one day I saw Patrick sitting with his hand over his chest, breathing through his mouth, a horrible rattly sound coming from him as the air went in and out. There was nothing I could do for him at home; he ended up spending two nights in Victoria Hospital. I took out thousands of rupees from the bank to pay for his bed, and it was not even a nice bed in a semi-private room; they put him in the general ward with germs going into his body from all the other sick people around him. And then the hospital told me he needed this injection and that special medicine, so I sold the necklace and the bracelets my mother and aunt had given to me when I had got married.

They had combined their money to buy the jewelry for me, the gifts for Patrick and his family, and the food for the guests. My father had said I could take anything from the house that I liked, and when I demurred, he unglued the carpet from the living room for us. They have been dead for so long now, and the small house in Soldier Bazaar and all the things inside it belong to other people.

After Patrick came home from the hospital, I said to myself, *Ruth, be practical. There is nothing in your locker in the bank. What are you going to do with all your hours of holidays?* I told my students that I was available to teach on all the days of the week. "Because you need the extra practice; next year are your final board exams, your O Levels. Tell your mothers, same fees as for regular classes," is what I said to them.

Nida's mother pays me sometimes, and other times she does not. She thinks that oh, that Mrs. Ruth is just a neighbor. But I am noting down in my book all the money that she owes me. Maybe one day it will be useful. I am also noting, in my mind, Nida's behavior in my classes. She sits with the boys at the back, never any girls. Tall, thin boys with collarbones and loosened ties. They like to talk to her even though she is not a beautiful girl. I don't know what kind of studying Mrs. Farzana thinks her daughter does during chemistry.

* * *

Patrick can get in a bad mood before I have to start teaching. He says to me, "Make me Chinese rice," or, "My eyes are hurting. Read me the newspaper." Nothing I can do when he gets like that. I cannot tell my students, "Go away now, please. I have to make soup for Mr. Patrick," or, "No class today, my husband needs me to read him the newspaper." When I teach, I give my students full attention. Sometimes some girls say to me, as they hand me my fees in little envelopes, "Oh, Mrs. Ruth, you are so nice, you always help us." And sometimes they give me small presents.

Kamila from downstairs also likes to give me a little something every now and then. One day it is half of a cake she has baked, another time it is kheer or biryani. She can make these kinds of food because she and her husband have a son, Rajeet, who lives in Malaysia and sends them money. Some weeks ago she let it slip that he had not sent them anything for a couple of months now. I like to help when I can; I put some money into her hands. If I could, I would be the only one giving.

Patrick's left elbow has become big like a tennis ball and he is not letting me see it.

"Does it hurt?" I ask.

No answer.

"Let me see it properly."

He picks up the remote control and turns on the TV.

I go downstairs to Kamila's flat to get arnica cream. She has not stepped out much recently. I wonder what I will say to her if she asks me for financial help. When she opens her door, I am surprised to see her face looking young and fresh, all the lines of worry on it disappeared. There is a big mess in her living room—books on tables, a dusty carton of dishes on the floor, suitcases open on sofas.

"Is Rajeet getting married?" I blurt.

Kamila presses her lips and smiles hard and her cheeks puff out like two small knobs. "I have some news to tell you. Rajeet's father and I are moving to Kuala Lumpur. We leave as soon as our paperwork is finalized."

I smile hard and say, "Congratulations. You will be so happy there." I do not make any sort of offer to help or pack, and do not promise to return the jar of arnica.

Patrick has not moved from his place in all the time I was gone; his eyes are still on the dumb TV. "I am back," I say very loudly, but he says nothing. In the kitchen I rip open a chamomile tea bag and the leaves scatter all over the counter. I gather them in a heap and beat them with a pestle, but they do not break up. I bring the pestle down even harder until there is an ache in my hand and the leaves have become smaller. I mix them with the arnica cream and spread it all on a piece of cotton. I go to where Patrick is and stand in front of the TV.

"Show me your elbow," I say to him like a schoolteacher, and he lets me wrap the cloth around the swelling.

Arnica has helenalin, I tell my students. One or two write it down, the rest look bored. Nida tilts her head to the boy on her right and he whispers something in her ear. Her mother owes me money for a whole month of Saturdays now.

Kamila is decluttering, she says. She gives me a planner that she says she never even opened, and a red clock. I do not know what to do with the month-by-month organizer since it is already November, but the maroon leather cover is nice. I put the clock on the dining table and give Kamila a slice of fruit cake. She has been a friend for a long time.

In the bathroom, I arrange a plastic stool for Patrick to sit on and a bucket of warm water with a jug so he can take his bath. I come back after thirty minutes with a towel so I can help him dry his hair and find him outside on the balcony in the cold night air.

"Come inside."

"You do not want me to get fresh air," he says. His thin hair moves in the wind. No jacket, no hat, not even a warm shirt. My own face has become covered with sweat.

"Patrick," I say, and he turns around finally. I cannot read his expression because it is dark outside. He walks slowly into the room. I go to him, making my smile nice and pleasant, and drape the towel around his shoulders.

But he catches a cold the next day, and soon he has a terrible cough which shakes his whole body. It comes all the way from his stomach, tearing its lining. I am sure it is tearing up his insides. I give him clove and honey drops, but they do not keep him settled for long. I help him inhale steam from hot water mixed with ground ginger and a pinch of cinnamon, and still he coughs almost half the night. For four days he does not eat anything, he does not watch his programs on TV, just stays on his bed with his eyes closed and his chest rising and falling slowly. I am not able to be a good teacher during this time. My students ask many questions and I am not able to give the correct answers. Kamila comes to visit and hears the terrible sounds from Patrick and tells me he needs to go see a doctor. On the fifth day I wait for his afternoon nap, then I pick up the red clock and touch its two little feet and the golden Roman numerals from one to twelve. I carry it to Mrs. Farzana's flat in an old gift bag. She opens the door only a little bit, her face peeking out suspiciously.

I say, "You are looking smart. The children are well? I got them a small gift, I hope they like it."

She slowly takes the bag and smiles, but it is very brief and very tight. "There was no need for this. This is so kind of you. The children are well, just preparing for their exams. And how are you and Mr. Patrick?"

I say, "Actually, he has been a little sick lately—"

"Yes, there is a nasty cold going around." Mrs. Farzana takes a small step back.

"He has to go see his doctor," I say in a rush. "And he is too unwell for the bus or the rickshaw, and you are the only one in the building with a driver—"

"I am so sorry to hear that, Mrs. Ruth. I am sure you can find a taxi which will take you to the hospital." Mrs. Farzana starts closing the door. "The children would be coming home now and I must see that lunch is ready. Goodbye."

I look at her big, brown door and think, *She took the clock.* My hand is trembling and I ring the bell but no one comes to the door. My face is hot with embarrassment and anger. My heart continues beating fast as I help Patrick down the stairs and into a taxi. I hear his breaths rattling in his chest next to me.

The taxi driver is most kind. He holds Patrick's elbow all the way into the hospital. I give him a tip of ten rupees. The doctor we see has gray hair, but he is younger than me. Maybe fifty-five. He nods occasionally while I speak, and he writes on his pad all the time. Then a nurse walks over in her big shoes and puts a syringe in Patrick's arm to draw blood. I do not understand what they are going to check. "Oh, deficiencies, Mrs. Ruth," the doctor says. "Iron, vitamins. Necessary at his age." He sends us home with a bottle of cough syrup and a packet of vitamins. At home I crush the big oval pill. In a cup of milk, I add a pinch of turmeric, a few crushed kalonji seeds and the medicine. Patrick says he does not like the color of the milk, but drinks it anyway. Perhaps he is tired.

I make my students write down: turmeric has curcumin, nigella has thymoquinone. Curcumin links with thymoquinone and sits on inflammations to bring them down.

"What do you mean "sits", Mrs. Ruth?" says the boy next to Nida. He has a half smile on his face; he is showing her he is clever and this teacher is an old, silly woman.

"Yes, sits," I say. "On its bottom. Like you sit on your bottom and make jokes."

Later I see Nida pass him a note, and he writes something

in the palm of her hand. She glances at me and does not move her hand away, even though she sees my red face.

Two days after this, I am coming back from buying groceries and I see Mrs. Farzana walking out of our building. Her little Suzuki is standing nearby, her driver behind the steering wheel. She keeps her head low and gets into the car very quickly. She has seen me, I am sure of it. The back of her head looks guilty. I am about to spit on the ground when I remember that she used to forget to lock her flat. It was a long time ago, when her Nida had just been born and there was no husband to help with the baby and she was so tired from not sleeping she used to forget a lot of things. Milk for her tea, diapers for the baby, payment for her phone bills. I decide to get my clock back.

My breath gets shorter with every step but I do not stop; I am going to walk right into her flat. But this time she has remembered to lock her door. I lift the welcome mat but there is no key under it. I turn the handle again and push the door with my shoulder but it only shakes in its frame. There is a noise on the other side.

"Who is it?" Nida says.

"It is me, Mrs. Ruth." My voice is high and thin.

"Hello, Mrs. Ruth. How are you?" She sounds unsure, perhaps a little afraid.

"I am fine, thank you. Can you please pass a message to your mother? It is about the clock she had borrowed, I would like it returned if she is done with it." Then I quickly add, "Mr. Patrick is very fond of it, you see."

"I will let her know. Goodbye."

I am almost certain there is relief in the girl's voice.

But Mrs. Farzana does not send the clock back. Her daughter enters my flat at class time, walks with her eyes down straight to her seat at the back of my drawing room. She lifts her head only when the boy she likes is sitting next to her. One afternoon that week she mumbles to me that she has to step out for a while, and three or four minutes later the boy follows. They do not come back to class that day.

Patrick's feet have become one-and-a-half times their size. I go out to buy him new, larger shoes while he is watching a documentary on TV about mangroves in Pakistan. The shoes are made of very good leather, almost half the cost of his blood pressure medicine. But the stubborn man insists upon squeezing his bloated feet into his old ones. "If you try to take it away, I will throw it at you," he says, holding his old shoe with both hands.

After every lesson, I send Nida home with a note for her mother. On Monday I write, "Mrs. Farzana, please return my property, that is, the red clock. Regards, Mrs. Ruth." On Tuesday it is, "I await the return of my red clock. Thanking you in advance, Mrs. Ruth." On Wednesday: "It has come to my notice that my red clock, which Mr. Patrick is very partial to, is still at your flat. Kindly return it via Nida." On Saturday I write, "I shall take swift action imminently to ensure the return of my clock. Mrs. Ruth." Each time, Nida takes the note from my hand without a word. I know she reads it the moment she leaves my flat, checking if I am telling her mother about her meetings with her boyfriend. Mrs. Farzana sends nothing back with her.

The nurse from the hospital calls and says Patrick needs to see the doctor for his blood test result. I hold the receiver with both hands and turn away from my students. I do not want them to hear. "But what is the result?"

"I cannot release it on the phone, ma'am," the nurse says.

"Please, it would be so kind if you tell me, it would help Mr. Patrick not worry, you see," I say.

Like a bleating sheep, the woman repeats, "I'm sorry, madam, I cannot tell the results on the phone. You will have to come see the doctor."

All evening, I look up my students' phone numbers and cancel the next day's tuitions. But I do not call Mrs. Farzana. Let Nida come to my door and ring and ring the bell. On Saturday morning, I help Patrick shave his gray stubble. I tell him stories to keep his mind away from the hospital. I tell him that I caught Ahsan passing a note to Maryam, and that Hamza got in trouble with his parents for being out past his curfew. I am sure all the names and situations are like a pot of porridge for Patrick. He cannot even tell one student apart from another. I manage to get his arms through the sleeves and reach toward the buttons, but he pushes my hands away.

"Come now, we don't want to be late," I say.

"Go," he says.

"Don't be unreasonable. This won't take long."

But he turns away from me, his fingers fumbling over the buttons.

There is no one in the building who will take Kamila's blue

bag in exchange for driving us to the hospital, so I find us a taxi, an old black one with the lower fare, not the newer yellow one. The whole way Patrick sits with his head in his hands like he has a headache or is tired of life or maybe me. The hospital is crowded and germs are everywhere in the waiting room. I find two empty chairs at the end of a row and I put Patrick on the one by the aisle so he is a little bit away from the line of sick people. Our turn comes after thirty long minutes, but the nurse who comes to get us does not say "Sorry to keep you waiting." We could have been waiting a week for all she cares. The doctor puts on a wide smile when he sees us, then spends a lot of minutes reading the report on his desk. I tell myself not to worry, I have done a good job preserving Patrick's health. Round-the-clock-care, like the poster on the wall says.

Finally, the doctor wags a finger and says, "Has your wife not been feeding you well, Mr. Patrick? This says here your vitamin D is low, but that is nothing alarming. I will give you something for the fever and the cough." He turns off his smile and starts writing on a prescription pad as if the topic is closed. But there are still questions in my mind.

"He has not been eating anything," I say.

The doctor puts his pen down, crosses his fingers on his desk, and closes his eyes.

I continue speaking anyway. "His cough is full of phlegm, and it goes on and on. It damages his stomach lining. You need to give him something to repair it."

The doctor opens his eyes and looks at me to make sure I am done talking, then he says, as if very kindly, "What is it that you do, Mrs. Ruth?"

I sit up very tall. "I am a chemistry teacher. I have been teaching for forty years, and I understand certain things about chemical reactions in the body."

"Ah, a school teacher. I should have guessed." He opens a thin folder, closes it, lifts a piece of paper and reads it. "There is nothing wrong with your husband's stomach lining."

Kamila gives me money before she and Mr. Aneet leave for the airport. She says it is a gift from one friend to another. I go to a pharmacy and buy paracetamol tablets, cough drops, and Vicks. I buy a syrup for weakness and a syrup for heartburn. I buy five packets of painkillers and a bottle of vitamins. I walk all the way back to my flat. In the kitchen, I put away in a cupboard my plastic packs of black seeds, ginger powder and anise; my foeniculum and syzygium aromaticum and chamomile; the tea bags which are not black tea. Even all together they do not take a lot of space. I arrange on the counter all the bottles and packets from the pharmacy.

A few days later Patrick falls down in the bathroom and hurts his hip, but there are no broken bones, only a very large, purple bruise. I wait for his fever, and when it comes I give him a tablet.

My students have their mock exams in school. Nida gets a C+. Mrs. Farzana marches into my drawing room and says I have done a poor job as a teacher. Her fingers poking the air are very bony, so different from the rest of her body which becomes wide like the letter A from her waist down. There is a dry spot under her lower lip. It does not look good. Nida stands behind her quietly. Her eyes are wide and her face, even her lips, are pale. She is thinking I will tell her mother about the boy, the notes with the hearts, all the bunked tuition classes, but I do not feel like saying anything. Soon, Mrs. Farzana gets tired and leaves, knocking over a book on her way.

It has become very windy now, and sometimes the temperature in the city goes to below fifteen degrees Celsius. I put an old towel in the crack under the balcony door in our bedroom to stop the air from coming inside. When the bruise on Patrick's hip fades, I take him for little walks, just to the end of the street and back. It is important for his circulation and nerves. I convince him to wear his sweater and woolen cap all the time. I talk to him about the neighbors. I tell him the newly married couple on the fifth floor went to Malaysia for their honeymoon, and that Mr. Anwar on the third floor refuses to get his doorbell fixed, which is why he missed the delivery of an important document. I don't know what things I say are true or untrue. It doesn't really matter.

Nida does not come to chemistry classes anymore. Maybe her mother sends her to a different place now. It doesn't matter. After she left, I got six new students and was able to get the bedroom painted. One evening I see her get out of a car that is not hers. There is a boy behind the steering wheel. I turn my face away, but she quickly steps up to me. She says hello and hands me a plastic bag. I look inside and see the red clock.

AN ACT OF CHARITY

AFTER AN HOUR IN the tunnel, Shahid's legs started to cramp. He had been in a crouch the whole time, worried about getting his pants dirty by sitting on the layer of rubbish there. He reached out a hand slowly, and even more slowly he brought his fingers down. He was afraid of feeling something damp, something soft, but it was dryness that he touched. Paper, or leaves, maybe. He shifted until his body was above his hand and lowered himself onto whatever it was that was not rotting wetly. He straightened his legs and, in the relief of the blood flowing, he sucked in his breath and the smell of dirty water from the open sewer made him choke. A breeze started to blow into the tunnel and he took off his shoes and socks and wiggled his toes in the air. A few more minutes went by, and then, overcome with tiredness, lulled by the breeze, he lay down completely, his head on his shoes. It was a little after midnight. From the road outside, the sound of the traffic had gone away; only the odd car whisper-rushed, or a truck sped by noisily. It was peaceful.

He closed his eyes and slept. When he awoke, the day had begun. He crawled out of the tunnel, went home, showered, and went to work.

———————————

A few weeks after this, he went with Mira to a party. The two of them had gotten engaged six months ago, when everything in Shahid's world seemed to be happening on schedule; when he could explain the restlessness inside him as just extra, unchallenged energy, so he had taken up running, then a new language, then the possibility of a different job. Mira sometimes laughed and said as long as he didn't take up an expensive hobby he could do whatever he liked. They had become best friends in college, and their engagement had been inevitable.

She laughed at something he said as they walked up to their friends' house. He had not told her about the tunnel.

The party was Rafi and Sara's one-year-wedding anniversary celebration. By the time Shahid and Mira arrived, dinner had been laid out. The guests were allowed to respond to their respective hungers and go to the main dining area as they pleased. For almost two hours the serving dishes—the ones elevated on metal stands with small candles underneath—were refilled as needed by the staff. In this crowd of people who had graduated only a few years ago, in these rooms full of comfortable pieces of furniture, under the flood of words from friends and acquaintances, everyone's faces lit up by soft yellow lights, Shahid felt warm and happy, and calmer than he had in a while. He felt connected to all of these people's dreams and hopes and ambitions. He felt concern when they brought up their parents' health, and when they discussed work performances and the anxiety of being bypassed at their companies for fast track lists to bigger roles. He was full of wordless admiration for Hina when she told him about her father's cancer treatments. He remembered, from what Mira had told him, that she worked almost around the clock and had two children now and her husband was a dull, successful person in the banking world. He was full of praise for Anisa who, after just one year as a trainee in a marketing department somewhere, had made a right-turn into the art world. He remembered she had always painted, large canvases of autumn trees with leaves covering the ground, and winter scenes of snow-covered limbs of other kinds of trees. For a while now she had been painting whirling dervishes.

"Have you been to Turkey?" Shahid had stupidly asked her last year, at someone's wedding, after Anisa had shown him a photo on her phone of her recently finished work. "No," she had replied. "These images come to me in a dream."

She showed him new photos at the anniversary party now. Shahid did not understand them; they seemed to him more like streaks of colors in a suggestion of figures and less like actual figures, or incongruent backgrounds of tall buildings or highways instead of the earlier, more peaceful blues and greens. He put his incomprehension down to a lack of understanding about art in general.

He wasn't even irritated by the things Ahmed said to him and Mira.

"Are you still stuck selling at that terrible detergent brand?" Ahmed asked.

Shahid nodded.

"And are you still saving lives or whatever it is you do at the Women's Welfare Association?"

Mira said, "It's great, so eye-opening, you know."

Shahid was proud of Mira for choosing to do the kind of tough work that her job asked for. Right here in these rooms were the very embodiments of reasons to want to live. Art, love, procreation. Even the easing of an elderly parent's life toward death was a reason to want to live. His night in the tunnel—and, before that, his running out of his office, driving recklessly, parking next to the sewer drain, and crawling into that space filled with garbage—all that seemed far away, like a dream.

By eleven o'clock, a few guests had gone home. The women who remained stood in corners in small groups, their talk more confidential now. The men sat on sofas, their exchanges also of a deeper kind, their laughter a little more ironic. There were jokes about commitment and death, old professors, new bosses, and the government. By half past eleven Shahid had laughed and commiserated and shaken his head so much his temples were beginning to hurt. He was jiggling a knee. He realized he was hungry, and he sat with that sensation for a little while, puzzled, because he thought he had eaten almost constantly since he had arrived at the party. He decided to find Mira. He hadn't seen her almost all evening. There had been a moment, earlier, when he thought she was standing by the table, looking at him, but when he got there she had left the spot. He was feeling tired now. The warmth that had grown inside him from being in the middle of sincere humans was dissipating now. He was remembering the tunnel again, the clarity he had received in there. He mumbled an excuse to the others near him. He started to walk from room to room, forging a narrow passage for himself through the eating, chatting people, looking for Mira. It had become more urgent that he talked to her. What was he going to say, though?

He found her talking to a female servant who was filling a tray with used dishes. Mira seemed to be offering her help but the woman kept refusing with a polite but forceful wave of her hand, and, eventually, she walked away determinedly, bearing her heavy tray all by herself.

"Do you think this table is beautiful?" Mira asked Shahid. "I think Sara got it custom-made." Then she sighed.

"You sound tired. Would you like to go home? It's getting late anyway."

"No, no, let's stay. It's nice to see all these people again. It's just... did you see that poor woman's clothes? So worn out."

"I've quit my job. Yesterday. I'm not with the detergent company anymore."

"You're changing jobs? When did that happen? Why didn't you tell me?"

"No, I'm not working at all. I'm not joining a different company. I don't want to."

"You don't want to work."

"No."

Mira looked at Shahid. "But you were doing so well. You told me. Last quarter's targets met and everything."

"Yes but I don't *want* to do that anymore." He took a deep breath to steady his voice but when he spoke again he sounded more excitable and irresponsible. "I don't want to make myself care about graphs about dirty clothes or focus groups about whether people like blue packaging or green." Mira was staring at him now, so he couldn't stop even if he'd wanted to. "Or active ingredients, or deadlines. Or performance reports."

"What about us? We're supposed to get married!"

Somebody from the drawing room wandered in just then, a friend of a friend. Shahid and Mira rearranged their expressions but the person grinned and said, "Ooh! Trouble. Don't worry, it all works out in the end." He gave them a thumbs up and retreated.

Mira picked up right away. "My money can only get us groceries. Are we going to live forever in your one bedroom apartment in Saddar?"

"There are other things that are so much more important than that, Mira."

Mira's eyes were wide and her nostrils flared. Shahid didn't think it was a look of anger. He chose to believe she was still surprised.

He said, "Do you remember years ago when we'd protested in front of the Press Club?"

"Yes, Shahid, I remember. It was, like you said, years ago."

"Do you remember how great that had felt? How purposeful?" He reached for Mira's hand but she jerked it away. "I want to get involved in life like that again. Be with actual people."

"I already do that," Mira said, trying to keep her voice low, but she was angry, so it came out thin and squeaky. "You're supposed to do what *you're* good at."

"But the things I'm good at don't matter."

At that moment the servant came back, her tray filled with clean glasses this time. Mira and Shahid became quiet again, watching the woman work. She glanced at them, set down the rest of the glasses hurriedly, and left.

"Do you hear how you sound?" Mira asked. "You've got a *degree*. You've got a *future*."

And now he was angry as well. Angry and misunderstood. "Do you know where I was a few nights ago? A tunnel. I left the office and spent the night inside this stinking, dirty place because it was better than another minute at my desk. And you know what else? I felt happy there. I *thought* about things. About our real purpose here. And how we need to live in a truer way, with courage and sacrifice. We should be where the refugees are, where the natural disasters are, and not cocooned from all that."

With a mixture of disbelief and resignation, Mira said, "I'm going to end up like that maid" and walked out of the room.

Shahid watched her go, suddenly deflated. His stomach growled and he looked confusedly toward the assembly of food on the table. He picked up a spring roll and ate it in two bites. Then he ate two more. His hunger appeased, some of the conviction he had felt that night in the tunnel came back to him. Once again, life seemed large and nebulous and exciting.

Searching for water, his mind still trying to mold his feelings into a shape he could explain to his fiancée, he went into the kitchen, and saw the maid washing dishes, her sleeves rolled up to her elbows. On her left was a pile of wet plates. She saw Shahid but did not say anything. He grabbed a dishcloth. "Let me help, please." He picked up a plate and dried it and found a place on the counter to set it down on. The maid glanced at him despairingly. "There's no need to, sir," she said, almost pleadingly.

"It's OK," he said, feeling more confident. "It's good to help. We're all the same."

In silence, they worked side by side. Shahid felt almost ebullient again. If there was any misery or discomfort emanating from the woman he did not feel it. He had dried six plates when suddenly the maid said, "Please, sir, I will do the work now." There was force in her voice. Shahid set down the dishcloth and gave a brief nod. His hands had begun to tire anyway.

"Well. Call me if you need any help. What's your name?"

"Noor."

He was wiping his hands on his jeans when the kitchen door opened and the host, Rafi, walked in with an empty plate in his hand.

"Hey! What the hell are you doing in here?" Rafi said. "Do you need anything? Coffee? Tea? Noor, bring us some coffee, please."

"I really don't want any, thanks," Shahid said.

They went back out together. The configuration of the people on the sofas had altered a bit. Now there were more of those who had gone to school with Rafi. There seemed to be an unspoken sense of togetherness among them. They occupied a continuous length of space. When Shahid appeared, they smiled at him and shifted, automatically making room for him, because he was one of them.

Back in school Rafi's house used to be called the Palace. Those in the circle whose parents had to save all their lives to be able to send their son or daughter to the best school and then the best university in the city—whose mothers had to choose which of their gold bracelets from their own long-ago weddings to sell to afford part of the tuition fee and which to keep for their child's future marriage, and whose fathers worried about telephone bills and car repair bills and the electricity bills in the summer when the one air-conditioner in the house was almost never off—they called Rafi's house the Palace, a place of refuge. There, they could leave dirty bowls piled in the sink, eat fistfuls of the cereal Rafi's father got for him on his travels to the US, have two air-conditioners on in two different rooms at the same time, do their homework in front of a music video channel where the skin and the makeup and the music would have sent their middle-class mothers and fathers into paroxysms of shock. There were a few in the group whose families had been luckier with wealth—modest investments made by a grandparent that comfortably cushioned the next two generations, or fathers who did exceptionally well at work, were ruthless and clever, had climbed the ladder of success, and proudly called themselves self-made. These boys and girls—one or two of them—called Rafi's house the Palace with a sense of irony. A sense of: "Our parents actually worked to get where they are but I suppose this world is meant to be unfair," because Rafi's family's wealth was of the old, inherited kind. There were mills involved, and farms outside the city, and buildings in the city, and rumor had it that half of an island belonged to them as well. All these facts were softened by two things: Rafi's house, though palatial and always the right temperature, was filled with old, slightly worn out things; and Rafi himself was a kind, quiet person who preferred to drive himself to school, and, later, to university and his internships and everywhere else, instead of having his driver drive him around.

Words and fragments of sentences drifted into and out of Shahid's consciousness. He tried to pay attention to what these people were saying; these were serious words. Confessions of frailty, of lack of confidence in new ventures. Someone mentioned an old incident—"Who was that boy who got accused of cheating in an exam?"—and they remembered his name eventually. Niyaz. A college friend—a later friend—asked, "What happened?"

The school friends shook their heads and gave low half-laughs which were not real laughs. Well, they began. It wasn't just because Niyaz wasn't a great student. Used to fall asleep during class sometimes. But, they continued, that teacher had never liked him anyway.

Goodness, the college friends breathed out. Why? Shahid frowned and nodded occasionally; he knew the story.

But he couldn't sit still anymore. Had Mira called a taxi and left?

She was in a small sitting room, staring at a painting of a Mughal hunting scene. "This is ugly," she said. "Where were you?"

"I was with the others," he said. He felt better because she had talked about a painting.

Mira crossed her arms. "Which tunnel was it?" she asked.

"The one across the road from my office."

A few seconds passed by in silence, then Mira said, "I asked Sara what those pretty red flowers in her garden were called and she said she didn't know, she never knows what her gardener plants. He just hands her a bill and she pays him whatever it says. I'm sure she doesn't even know when she runs out of milk.

It all just—happens. Do you know, she and Rafi are going to have a baby. It will be here in December. Just as she'd planned, she told me." She paused, then said, "Have you thought about your mother?"

Shahid thought about his mother, who lived in another, smaller city. She had been a widow for almost eight years now and had long looked forward to the day her son would go out into the world and earn the living that was sorely needed to ease her financial burdens. He also had a little sister who was finishing school, and even as he found his work increasingly burdensome to his spirit, he had kept sending them money, and those women in his life had kept thanking him and recounting to him the many, many uses that money had.

Sometimes, Shahid wondered if the proof of the worth of his existence was that he woke up from every sleep. He knew what happened to souls at night; while bodies slept, the souls left them and rose up to God. If the person was meant to have another group of hours—a day, a week, months or years of them—their soul would return to their body and the person would open their eyes. Of course, there were other ways to depart. When he was a child, he used to be afraid that his aunt, a person of volatile moods, would shoot his mother and father and her own mother too. It was a scary thought, but a little bit exciting. He did not think about death in a morbid way; he did not find it morbid. He did not wish for it, did not want to hurry it up. (About what happened *after* death all he knew was that angels visited one in the grave, after which there was to be a resurrection and a reckoning.) When he thought about not existing on Earth, it was by way of examining his life in contrast to an un-life. Who would miss him? And for how long? His parents, his fiancée, his close friends. Was there someone's life he had touched who would come to know of his passing and feel a pang of sadness? He had once heard a story of a woman who, every week, went to the house of an elderly couple to try to sell them plastic combs. The wife always shooed her away, but the husband always went after the woman and bought a comb. Later, when the husband died, the comb-seller sat on the ground and cried and cried. The wife, astonished, asked the woman what was wrong. The woman said, "He was a very kind person." Shahid wanted a stranger to become dissolved with grief over his absence.

"I have some ideas…" he began now, but he could not continue because he saw Mira caressing the engraving in the wrought iron column of a lamp. His eyes went to the heavy base, also full of patterns, making an indentation in the carpet. He knew nothing about carpets—his own one-bedroom apartment had only a thin one—and he wondered if Rafi and Sara knew how many square feet of carpeting their home had. The only time Shahid's shoes had touched bare floor in their house was in the kitchen. Even there the tiles seemed to have an unstainable quality. And here was Mira, wearing shoes with no heels; toenails with no nail polish sticking out of them; her hair, cut in a plain style, dull after a hard day's work with sad women. He imagined her looking more and more worn out each year, scrubbing dishes the way he had seen the maid do if they could not afford to hire help.

"Look," he said. "I know I must do the getting up, the going to work, doing something sensible and maybe worthwhile. The bringing home the—the being the foundation and the pillars and the roof of our future family. I'll go back to my job."

Mira looked up. "You're clever with your work. If you just keep doing it then I can keep doing the only thing *I'm* good at. We will flourish, you'll see. And, after a few years, you can look at other options, right?"

Shahid nodded, tired now, feeling as if a great fever had left him. The maid entered the room they were in and began to collect cups and mugs from various surfaces. Shahid supposed she was good at that, though there was nothing glorious about it, nothing she would be remembered by.

He murmured, "What a life."

Mira saw where he was looking and said in a whisper, "It's appalling how Rafi and Sara treat her."

She had misunderstood him. He said, "What? No. Rafi's so humble, he'd never mistreat anyone."

"It's his wife Sara. She told me she'd loaned the maid money for her younger sister's treatment or wedding or something. Now the poor woman can't even just get up and quit."

"Well. That's definitely not good."

"We've got to get that maid out of here."

"Sure, we could drop her home. Too late for a bus."

"That's not what I mean. Every day that she works in a house like this she's reminded of the wasteful, luxurious ways of a tiny percentage of humanity. Let's do a good, meaningful thing. Let's rescue her."

"OK. Yes." Shahid nodded hard. Mira was right. Rafi was a good, simple person who used to iron his own shirts and then had married a woman who thought nothing of keeping a maid up late because of guests.

Mira had already left the painting. Shahid followed. In the kitchen they saw Noor dragging a five-gallon water bottle across the floor toward the dispenser. Shahid watched, his heart beating fast, as Mira strode over and gently put her hand over Noor's.

"It's past midnight. Aren't you tired?" she said.

"It's OK, madam," Noor said.

Mira made her voice lower. "They don't pay you well, do they?" Noor's eyes, red with sleep, became big. "Sir and madam are good people."

Mira took Noor's hands in her own. "They're some of the best. But look, you've been working all day and now you're lugging heavy bottles and cleaning up while sir and madam sit around and laugh with their friends." Mira paused and turned her head slightly in the direction of the drawing room. A second later, a peal of laughter came all the way into the kitchen, the unmistakable sound of Sara's mirth. This was followed by a deeper guffaw from Rafi.

Mira turned back to the maid. "We can get you out of here. We can take you to your house. With your skills you could be earning double, triple, more than what you're earning right now."

"I could recommend you to some people I know," Shahid said, not sure whom he had in mind.

"But what will I say to sir? And madam?" Noor said.

"You won't have to explain anything to sir."

"Nobody should have to live like a slave. You are worth more than this," Mira said. "I'll help you pack. Where's your room?"

Her indignation proved convincing, and Noor pointed

toward a small, dark corridor at the back of the kitchen. Mira took her elbow and Shahid followed slowly, not sure if he should, but wanting to very much. The maid's room was small, a single bed and a dresser taking up most of the space. He stood outside, watching Mira pull out a small suitcase from under Noor's bed and fill it with clothes from her dresser. From the top drawer, she took out a jar of face cream, a comb, and a small bottle of perfume and packed them.

"You've seen madam's dressing table, right? When you go to dust it?" she asked. "I'm sure it's crowded with at least ten bottles of perfume, three hairbrushes, and things she's forgotten about in all those drawers. And she probably keeps her jewelry locked somewhere in there, away from servants."

That was clever of Mira, Shahid could see. On Noor's face, her tiredness and nascent feelings of injustice solidified into a simmering anger. She said, "I am not a thief. If after all these years of faithful service madam cannot trust me, then there is no point in me staying here. I am ready to go."

Mira zipped up the suitcase and handed it to Shahid. It weighed so little that he felt a pang of real pity for the woman. She owned so little. He pressed his lips; they were doing the right thing. Mira covered Noor up with a shawl and they left quietly through the kitchen door. They walked past the guard at the main gate, down the street to where Shahid had parked his car. He fumbled in his pocket for the key and thought, *I was last here yesterday.* He knew it was an absurd thought, like saying, "I'll see you next year!" on New Year's Eve, as if next year were months away. But at that hour, with the street completely quiet except for the sounds of Mira and Noor's shoes hurrying toward him, he felt as if an age had gone by since he had arrived.

They established Noor in the back seat with her small suitcase next to her. "She lives in Akhtar Colony," Mira told Shahid. "Lock your doors." He started the car, and soon Rafi and Sara's well-lit, colonnaded house was behind them. Shahid wanted to say something celebratory to the maid but he could not decide upon the correct sequence of words in his head. Eventually he said, "Congratulations!" but he was so aghast at how flippant he sounded that he fell quiet.

Mira asked Noor, "Who lives in your home?"

"Only my mother and little sisters, madam. I have three sisters."

"Do they go to school?"

"Yes, madam," Noor said with some pride. "All three. I've always put all my money for their education."

Shahid vowed to himself to supply generous amounts of cash to Noor for as long as she needed. There was silence for a long time in the car. Noor told Shahid where to turn left and where to go straight. They reached a very narrow alley and Noor said that's where her house was. Shahid stopped the car but kept the engine running.

"Is it far from here?" Mira asked.

"Only the sixth one on the right." Noor's voice sounded small.

Shahid reached for his wallet and pulled out a few notes. "Here. Take these." Mira unwrapped her scarf from around her neck and put it in Noor's hands. Shahid took off his watch and put it on top of the scarf. Mira found a tiny bottle of perfume in her bag and added it to the other things.

"You are too kind, both of you." Noor's voice had tears. "God bless you and your children, your families, forever and ever." She made a neat bundle of her presents, tying the corners of Mira's scarf. She had some difficulty getting out and then pulling the suitcase off the seat. Shahid wondered if he ought to help her but he could not move from his seat; the street was so dark and the area so unsafe, so unknown to him. He sat hunched forward, holding the steering with both hands. Eventually, Noor managed to get out of the car with her belongings. She turned toward the dark alley and began to walk. Soon, Mira and Shahid could only make out her faint outline. They heard her knock on a metal door, low and hesitant. They waited for it to open, Noor and Mira and Shahid. The two in the car thought, *Would she be let in? Was her house a place where she would be forced to keep out? Where would they take her? What would their friends say? Would Rafi and Sara find out what they'd done?* After two or three minutes, the door creaked open and Noor stepped through it, and the door shut.

"Well," Shahid said, releasing his breath. "We stole our friends' maid."

"We saved her. We did something better than anyone else there tonight. We did an act of charity."

He supposed that that's what they had done.

When Shahid reached Mira's house, she got out of the car and said to him through the window, "You know, I bet we'd be much nicer to our maid."

Inside his apartment, he changed his clothes and brushed his teeth. He put away two books from a chair to a shelf. He hung his towel on the back of the chair. He brought a pencil into alignment with a pen. He pulled back the curtain a little. Other windows were still unlit. In a couple of hours, people would wake up and eat and get dressed. They would say goodbye and hello and climb into and out of cars and buses and fill the roads and then empty them. They would do this every day.

THE LEAVERS

RAZA SITS ON THE bench next to me and shows me the sports section of the newspaper he's been reading all morning. The newspaper is at least two decades old. He talks in a jerky manner about Germany and Holland and who won what match and why they lost until he interrupts himself, touches his small mustache, falters more and more until he stops, as if he realizes that he's heard himself talk about this very thing several times before. Then he explains to me why he hadn't done well in his grade nine exams. He is thirty-eight years old and can recall bad grades and the names of his enemies from his school days.

I stop listening. Outside, the sun burns strong, but inside, all the lights are switched on. There are no windows in this part of the hospital—where the patients roam, their minds rearranged from treatments that remove voices and visions that only they can hear and see. When I watch them here, I feel obscene about my healthy male body in my ironed scrubs, my nurse's arms strong from helping their uncertain bodies. I wonder what their family and friends feel—guilt or grief. When they leave they have their arms wrapped around themselves, or their mouths stretched in a too-tight smile. A while back, a mother walked out after visiting her son, her hands pressed against her stomach.

No one comes to see Raza. His older sister brought him in eight months ago and she hasn't returned since. There is no other family member listed in his file. When there is an unusual number of visitors for other patients, Raza is left all by himself on his small alien planet, hunched over and shuffling from corner to corner. I try to busy myself with paperwork, but his large, sad figure hovers in the periphery of my conscience—the conscience that should be his sister's. I feel irritable and angry, and I take him downstairs to the cafeteria and let him fill himself up with whatever he wants, and listen to him talk with food in his mouth.

Last week, the head nurse told us that Raza's sister called to say she's coming to see him in a few days. The head nurse advised us to not tell him in case, yet again, the sister doesn't show up. Part of me wants to tell him; perhaps the weight of his disappointment will crush him enough that he finally sees her as the selfish liar she is. She has always given excuses for canceling her visits—her health, her work, the family. It's been four days since her call. I find myself looking at the clock, though I try not to because it makes my blood pound behind my ears.

Every afternoon I send Raza to bed for a nap so that if she does visit, she will find him sleeping.

On the sixth day, the phone at the nurses' station rings. The sister has made it after all.

I watch her come down the corridor, walking deferentially behind the head nurse, perhaps because she thinks it's appropriate to appear humble. The fluorescent glare from the ceiling turns her skin the same shade as that of the patients. I can't unfold my arms from across my chest.

The day she had brought Raza to the hospital, he'd tried to bargain with her, telling her to take him back, that he would go to the doctors and the therapists, and he was never, ever going to scream at anyone in the street again, not even the man who sold shoes out of a box and kept a gun hidden in his pants pocket so he could put a bullet in Raza one day. He lunged to grab his sister's silk sleeve, and she pushed him off and yelled, "Won't someone get him?" A nurse got hold of Raza, and the sister straightened her clothes. "He cannot stay at home," she explained loudly and clearly to the nurse. Turning to her brother, she told him that he had six months to complete at the hospital and then he could go wherever he wanted, anywhere in the world, or he could stay in Karachi until he died and be buried by the sea or near the hills, wherever he chose; he could be whatever he wanted and do whatever he pleased. Didn't he remember all the things he wanted from when he was younger, years and hellish years ago? She waved to him from the safety of the other side of the ward door and left.

She doesn't look the same as that time—her clothes are ugly, drab and colorless, her hair dull and grayer. Her decline fills me with satisfaction. Above her crepe-skinned neck is her face with a tight smile on it. Her glance skips like a pebble from the surface of one vacant face to another. I see the men the way she must—their mouths a little down at the corners, eyelids drooping, hair unkempt. Some appear to say hello, but their waves are vague and unsure. They don't move fast, and the relentlessly brisk forward motion of the nurse and Raza's sister makes them appear extraordinarily slow. For a moment, I feel embarrassed for them.

The nurse stops in front of me and says to Raza's sister, "This is Murad. He's the one who usually looks after Raza. He has to give him his medication now."

Together we walk to a closed door. I have learned not to stride into this room where the men sleep. This is a dimly lit land of tenuous consciousness and soft breathing. There is a mound on each metal bed, not stretched out but huddled. I set the pills and water down on Raza's bedside table. His eyes are closed, but I know he is only gliding on the surface of sleep because his breathing is shallow. *Has the sister slipped out?* I wonder. I imagine running after her and hauling her by her hair from room to room, screaming into her ear. *This is where he was taken for electroshock therapy! This is where he walks from corner to corner every day! This is where he sits and talks for an hour while I only pretend to listen!*

"Are you sure this is OK? To wake him up like this?" It is her, whispering; she has crept closer to the bed. In the muted lighting her dilated eyes fill her face.

"You heard the nurse," I say.

"Of course," she nods. "I haven't seen him in a long time, you know."

I turn my back to her and give Raza's shoulder a gentle shake. He stirs and slowly sits up. A slight smell of sweat rises with him. His face appears swollen, his eyelids heavy. His hair is neatly parted, even after his sleep. Behind me, his sister gasps. I give him a moment to wake up while he looks at his bed, at a wall, at the plastic bowl and cup in my hands.

"Time for your medicine," I say with cheerful firmness.

Conditioned after hours and weeks and months of hearing this, he takes the pills and the water, swallows, and returns the cup.

"Good job," I say. "Now open your mouth so we can see if you've been good."

Dutifully, Raza opens his mouth and lifts his tongue and there is nothing hidden there.

I pat his shoulder. "Look who's here to see you!"

His sister steps forward and speaks to him in a low voice, almost a whisper. She is going to take him home soon, away from this place, she says. She chokes down some tears.

I go back to my apartment after my shift, unlock my door, and am met with an emptiness so solid it presses down on my lungs. There is a letter on the table, sent by my wife. It had arrived this morning. It looks pathetic lying there, as if it, like her, is wondering what I intend to do about the pair of us. I tear off the top of the envelope and skim the lines. She has filled the paper with more words than usual, questions crammed between questions. Am I alright on my own? Is my work long and hard? Do I miss her and home? It's been a long time since I left, saying that it was for her own good, but she hasn't been good. She never said I should leave, so why did I? She hadn't minded the smashed vase or the million shards of glass from the mirror I punched. She hasn't bought new glass for the frame because maybe I'd like to choose a new mirror altogether. There are sales in some furniture stores now. Could I come back so we could go shopping together? Did I know that I was a liar? The devil disguised as a healer?

I shove the letter under a cushion and go outside. I tell myself that I need food. The sun has just set and the city looks dirty in this light. I try to memorize each face I pass to replace hers, long with long eyelashes, and the memories of how she eats, sweats, flinches, talks. I make sure to walk in dirt where I find it. I give money to an old woman begging on a corner, and when I go home I eat a piece of old bread and go to bed hungry. That is OK. That feels right.

Raza's sister visits again, and I watch them have lunch in the cafeteria. I can't hear what she says but whatever it is, he answers steadily in short sentences in his low, rumbly voice. He keeps glancing at the way his older sister uses her fork and knife to cut up small bites and put them neatly inside her dry, thin-lipped mouth. Sometimes he sets down his fork and picks it up again and mutters. She leans forward with an attentive smile, the way a kindergarten teacher would. I wish he'd put on his only but-ton-down shirt, but he'd refused, choosing instead his old XXL pullover. The plastic cafeteria chair is a tight fit for him, but I've taught him how to press down on the arms to get out more easily.

His sister reaches into her large bag and takes out a green book. Raza holds it in his fleshy hands, opens it to a random page, scratches his neck and cheeks. He starts sentences and breaks off in the middle. I know the signs; he is getting agitated.

The visit has gone on for too long. I get up and tell his sister that it is time for his afternoon nap. She does not argue with my authority, and, with a feeling of satisfaction, I take him away from the mess of torn ketchup packets squeezed empty and crumpled, red-stained tissues; away from the presence of that failed woman who is his only family. On the way to the ward, he shows me what she has given him—a book of short prayers.

"She got this from a learned man, a very wise man. He doesn't see just anyone, you know. But he saw her," Raza tells me. There is pride in his voice.

Silently, I hand him his medicine and he swallows it, allows me to check his mouth, and puts his head on his pillow, the book tucked under it.

If she takes him home, would she know how to talk to him? Would she know about all the things that are forbidden, an impatient sigh, a slightly raised voice, a too-bright smile? Would she worry that the lights in her house are too similar to the lights in the hospital? Would she lock her door, then lie awake worrying that her brother could die of negligence if she doesn't hear him call out for help in the dead of night? Would she wait until sleep couldn't be put off any longer before she allows herself to drift away?

At night, lying on my couch, I remember that my wife collected books and placed them alphabetically on shelves. One day, after an argument, I'd pulled one from the shelf and thrown it against a wall, cracking the spine. I bought her another copy, but she never added it to her collection.

I turn up the volume of the TV, and it fills my apartment with comforting sounds, just like it does every night.

They always meet in the cafeteria. Sometimes his sister brings him bananas, sometimes clothes. When he wants to eat a burger with fries, she tells him that he must not be greedy with his food.

"We must fill our hours with good things," I hear her tell him once. "It's the only guaranteed way to keep away the devil and all the bad thoughts that he brings."

"Well, I try, I think," Raza says, staring at his lap. "I mean, it is hard, in a place like this, full of people from all over, with their secret plans."

"Nobody's planning anything." His sister's voice is sharp. "You must not think bad thoughts about others. That's another sign of too much rich food."

He asks her to buy him a fancy watch and she says, "Look at me. Do I look fancy? I've never been happier since the day I let go of false ways to feel better. I'll get you a strong, plain watch."

She brings him a watch with a black strap and a dial which tells nothing but the time, and it is not like the kind he'd seen on the wrist of a kid when he was in grade seven. She also brings him a prayer rug.

Raza asks me where he can find a good place to set it down. "My sister said it's a good idea to pray," he says. "She prays a lot. She's a good person." He stands hunched before me, passing his fingers over his mustache, his glance going from my left shoulder to my right one.

I feel pity and a twinge of disdain toward him for giving her this unearned pedestal. I wonder if she takes antidepressants after every visit.

"You haven't prayed in years," I say, mockingly.

He gives an awkward laugh and scratches the back of his neck. "I thought I might try it. She says it helps her. I thought I'd try."

His ineloquence deflates my anger. I lay his rug in a corner of the rec room. From the doorway, I watch him place his feet on it and kneel. His hands self-consciously go up to his ears. His gravelly voice declares God's greatness, and there is a note of desperation in his tone. He sneaks a look to his left and folds and unfolds his fingers before settling them over his navel. "God is the greatest," I hear him whisper over and over and then he presses his forehead against the rug. Does he remember the rest of the words? I feel exhausted. I can't watch his jittery movements any longer. My shift has come to an end and I want to go home.

Sitting on my couch, I eat a sandwich I'd made in the morning and forgotten about. I chew slowly through the hardened bread and ten minutes go by. I decide to read but I cannot get comfortable. The tear in the cushion behind me bothers me. I think about the box that I know is on the floor, hidden in the shadow of the couch. My wife had sent it some time ago. I had put it where it wouldn't be easily seen. I throw down the book and pick up the box. There are photographs inside; the two of us at weddings and in restaurants, sometimes with friends, sometimes not. In each picture she and I are smiling. Echoes from a distant time. There is also a letter. I read it quickly, wanting to stay on the surface of her words. She sounds softer, as if, when she sat down to write, she was spent by her sulfurous eruption last time. She says that faith keeps her going, and some days, she does not mind waiting for me at all. She bears me no grudges. She believes that one day we will be good together. It is good to believe, she writes, because she feels stronger for it. At the bottom of the box are three bars of chocolate, gone soft over time. I put them in a bag to give to Raza and crawl into bed.

The head nurse tells me Raza is getting better and his sister wants to take him home next week. I digest this information, nodding as a detached professional should, biting the insides of my mouth. Raza does look better. His eyes used to have dark pouches under them, like small bananas going bad. He has started exercising on the treadmill in the rec room, walking on it heavily and slowly while a male attendant hovers nearby. He talks more coherently, mainly about things his sister has said. One evening he asks me if I ever worry about my soul, and my jaw tightens with anger but I laugh and say nothing. He tells me that he will pray for my guidance.

Guidance. That is a word I remember my wife using. She said she was seeking guidance because really, what else was there for her to do? She said this might be the most character-forming phase in her life yet, and she had me to thank for it.

If I don't go back to her, if I leave her alone, what then?

Would she wither or would she thrive? Perhaps, after a period of sadness, unnecessarily prolonged because bad habits are hard to break, she would discover that she knew the way out of the terrible maze of our marriage. She could pack her things into suitcases and boxes and take herself somewhere new, leave the broken bits of glass behind, leave my hair in my comb, my flakes of skin on my side of the bed. To make her feel better, I could promise her to faithfully stay alone, to return every night to my broken couch. A deserving arrangement.

The TV lulls me to sleep and then wakes me up. *Is Raza's sister on her prayer rug this time of the night, saving her soul?* With every visit to her brother she grows larger and smugger, certain of redemption. She forgets that she left her brother alone in this place, wandering in and out of rooms and states of mind. But Raza trusts her completely, frustratingly. He will allow himself to be taken home, to commit the ultimate act of forgiveness.

The day of Raza's removal from the hospital, his sister arrives early. She has brought small boxes of chocolates for the staff and is tearful as she thanks the head nurse. She wants to come with me when I go to wake up Raza. I cannot return her deferential smile. He is groggy and puts the pills in his mouth and then sits like a shapeless rock on his bed, refusing to swallow them. I haven't slept well and I am short with him. "Spit them out, then." He does, and they land in a small wet gob by my feet. His sister makes a sound—a gasp or a shudder or a whimper, I cannot tell. I scoop up the disintegrating pills and hold them up to her face. She is pale in the gloom. A coward, just like me.

I smile at her. "Are you sure you want to take him home now? You can still go back. No one will say anything. It happens all the time, really. Look, he's sleepy; he won't even know."

She steps past me and sits on Raza's bed. She takes out a piece of bread from her bag and hands it to him. "Eat this," she says, and he takes a nibble. "Have you been doing your good deeds?" she asks him, and just like that I am an outsider. "You want to get better and come home, don't you?" she says to him. "You must do your part. Good deeds wipe away all bad things, like this." She sweeps her hand over the bedcover and a smattering of crumbs falls off.

I stand by a wall and count the tiles on the floor. Some minutes later, they are ready to leave.

I stay in my apartment, hating the feel of the outside air on my head, on my arms. The head nurse from the hospital calls and says it's been five days since I went to work. I tell her I will not be going back. Because, I say to myself after I hang up the phone, how can I? I am not real there. I know that now.

I lift the cushions off the couch and pick up sheets of my wife's letters, pressed flat by all the hours I've lain there. "If we close our eyes and open them again, we can pretend to go as far back as we like." She'd said that one evening as we'd eaten toast among broken ceramic.

The TV is on and its images reflect mutely on the night-dark glass of the window. Now there is an indistinct picture of me on it, holding a phone to my ear and counting the rings.

WHAT'S FAIR?

THE DIFFERENCE BETWEEN ME and Afzal, I tell him, is that he has a greater need for things. Friendship, money, food. He wants a lot of all of those. He says, "You *think* you're different but you're the same as me." I start to disagree but then my phone buzzes. Samar Aunty has sent me a message. She says she wants: one pack of Panadol, one GoGo supari, and the three-piece pack of Femina Sanitary Napkins. The last item makes me groan. Afzal and I go to the shop, and we're lucky that it's the shopkeeper and not his son who is at the register. The shopkeeper knows not to change his expression when I tell him what I need and who the things are for, and when I say that he's to add it to Samar Aunty's weekly bill. He puts the napkins in a brown envelope, and all the things in a small plastic bag.

"How long will she need those for, you think?" Afzal asks, outside the shop.

"I don't know. How old is she? Forty? Fifty? Maybe she'll need them forever."

We make our way by the nullah and into Samar Aunty's lane. She gives me two rupees for the errand. She says, "I have a job today."

"Where?" I ask.

"A house in Gulshan. One of my regulars. The woman's getting a little comfortable leaving her cash around. That's all I'm telling you." Then she adds, "There's another one Munnoo has been hinting about. I'll talk to him about letting the two of you come along then. Bigger house, a wedding a month away."

Before we leave, she pushes two rupees into Afzal's hand as well. Once we are out of her neighborhood, he shakes his head. "What does she think this is going to get us?"

"Nothing, really. But keep it. Don't give it to your sister."

At my house, Mami says I am late. I had kept her son waiting for a full hour and a half and now he's gone to bed and he isn't going to do well on his test tomorrow. I say I am sorry. I don't ask her for food; she isn't going to give me any now. The floor is covered with my sleeping cousins. I climb over them to the doubled-up quilt in a corner and close my eyes. My body is tired but my mind stays awake. I want Munnoo to give me more work. I have been training long enough. The small-time jobs Afzal and I are stuck with are too easy now; sneaking wallets out of pockets, holding a toy gun to a lady in a bazaar and asking for cash which never gets us more than two hundred rupees, no matter where in the city we are. Munnoo says we lose our shit too easily and the women can sense that. Besides, we *look* fifteen even though we are nineteen. I hate it when he goes on like that. I tell him, "You wouldn't be keeping us around if you didn't need us, so the next big assignment is ours," and he says, "Keep growing that beard and maybe in six months you will be promoted."

Afzal and I meet at the bus stop. We have decided to try Bank Road today. I am starving by the time we get there. I had slept late and woken up angry at Mami and the cousin who couldn't remember his times tables. When Mami said to come eat, I told her I wasn't hungry. I left without wishing the cousin good luck for his test. At the market, I get a glass of sugarcane juice and it eases the ache and gets rid of the fog in the brain. I leave a third of the juice for Afzal; he isn't talking much and he looks pale and a little distracted. I think, *He really needs to get out of his sister's house.* It is a little after eleven. People are moving up and down the sidewalks and between parked motorbikes and cars.

"OK, should we split up? Or just start walking?" I ask Afzal.

"How about there?" He points with his chin toward a building across the road. It looks like there is a single gate for entrance, and the guard waving streams of people in and out seems tired already.

We spend five minutes there, and then we move on to another place, a bank this time, and another one. By two o'clock we have five wallets. It is a good time to take a break. I find three thousand rupees in the first one. It's just downhill after that. No more than a hundred or two in each.

"We won't have anything left after Munnoo's cut. We should take the credit cards," Afzal says.

"Not worth it. They'll get blocked and we could get tracked."

"Half of the money then."

He sounds upset.

"OK, one day, it's just not wise to piss Munnoo off this early in our careers."

We buy lunch from a stall. I tell Afzal that I think we're good for the day. "You could call Erum. She could meet you at the beach. And maybe her cousin could come along too. I can't remember her name. She has a nose ring."

"I'm not really in the mood today."

"What's the matter with you? How bad did it get with your sister last night? I thought her husband had hidden the belt?"

"He did. But she'll probably find something else."

"I don't understand why you don't move out. Saleem's going to get tired of saving your skin. Even sleeping in a drain has to be better than living with that witch."

Munnoo's office is just a part of a room in his house with a curtain drawn across. Afzal and I have kept a little money for ourselves, hidden in pockets inside our kurtas. Not half, but enough to keep us fed and our girls fed. I'm sure he knows that we don't turn in everything we find—probably everyone on his team does this—but he's never checked.

Afzal and I stand in front of him as he counts the cash across the table. He peels off a two hundred rupee note and hands it to us. "Well done," he says. "Well done, well done, well done. How's that chin hair doing?" He peers at my face. "I might have to promote you sooner than I thought."

We step outside the office. I feel the money burning in my pocket. I make Afzal call Erum and she says yes, she'll meet us at the park. I take the phone from him and ask her if she could bring her cousin and she says she will. "The one with the nose ring," I add quickly.

Afzal doesn't talk a lot on the way but I've got other things on my mind. At the park, he and Erum sit on a bench far away, leaving me with the cousin. I still don't know her name and I wish Erum had mentioned it. I want to sit with her on a bench as well but she says she's in the mood for a walk. I don't know if that means I can't hold her hand just yet. A minute into our stroll, she folds her arms below her chest, so at least now I know. After just one round she says she's hungry and walks over to Erum and lets her know. The girls start walking together to the gate and Afzal and I follow. We buy the girls burgers. They eat while talking about some family function. And then they say they have to leave because it is almost dark. I watch them go. Afzal and I walk back in silence. This whole evening has been useless. Erum's cousin hadn't looked like she was having a good time. And now, Afzal's sad, preoccupied face is making me irritated. I want to beat him up but I can't because his sister does it anyway and I don't want to be like her.

He says, "Saleem told me my father works in Lunda Bazaar."

I stop walking.

"How does *he* know?"

"He said he saw him—abba—himself. Last week."

"Does your sister know?"

"He hasn't told her."

"Do you want to see him?"

"I don't know. Maybe."

I breathe out slowly and rub my forehead. "If you ask me, this doesn't sound like a good idea."

All Afzal says to that is he should be getting back now.

For a while, I roam around by myself. It is the weekend and the food stalls are open. Families are eating and shopping. I wonder if I should try getting a wallet on my own. I begin to close in on a man walking toward the line in front of the Broast Chicken restaurant. Then his mobile rings, and I lose interest and turn away.

———————

Afzal has been to see his father. He saw him in a shop, selling used jeans and shirts, but he did not talk to him.

I ask him, "Is he old? Does he look like you?"

"Not old. A little like me, I think."

"You sure you saw the right man?"

Afzal makes an impatient sound. "Of course."

I have my doubts but I don't say anything. His sister has hurt her back so he has to help out at home. I don't have any work today. In fact, it's been five days since Munnoo has asked me to do anything. Around eight at night, I go to see Samar Aunty. That's when she's back from the house she cleans. I ask her about that big job she'd mentioned. She's tired and not in the mood to discuss it.

"It's for Afzal," I tell her. "He's upset about his father—you know how he left his family when Afzal was only two? Afzal found him a few days ago."

"The poor boy. Did he speak to him?"

"No. But he's become really moody since then. I would say he has depression."

"Mmm." Samar Aunty shakes her head. "I know about that. That is a hard thing to live with."

"I think this new job would help him. Keep him away from his sister, give him back an interest in life."

"OK, yes, I will speak to Munnoo. But it's not an easy assignment, nothing like slipping out a wallet and then hiding in the crowd."

"You can trust us, Samar Aunty, honest to God."

In another five days, she gets permission to include me and Afzal. I tell him what we're going to do. Even though I had lied a little to Samar Aunty about his condition, he really does look more excited than he has lately. The job is one week away, and we have preparations to make.

When we next see Munnoo, we thank him and ask him for something to do in the meanwhile, a small job, eight thousand rupees, no problem. But he says we should rest. Back in the street, Afzal says the two of us should go to Lunda Bazaar and do some light work there. I cannot believe he is even trying to lie.

I say to him, "You want to see your abba. Just say that."

"Yes, fine, maybe. But mostly I want to go there to get some money."

It is insulting how he persists with the pretense.

But we can't go there on Monday because my Mami keeps me tied up with chores all day, setting me free only in the evening. There is no time to do anything else so Afzal and I go to the park to practice running. This is for the job. Samar Aunty said we have to be in good shape; we might have to make a run for it. This is what she has told us will happen: she will use the key copy she has made to get inside the house; Afzal and I will slip in through the unlocked door sometime later; in twenty minutes, we will gather the things into bags; Munnoo will be outside with a car.

On Tuesday, we go to Lunda Bazaar. Now that we're here, Afzal doesn't waste any time pretending. He maneuvers through the mass of people until he stops by a wall. He says in a low voice, "That's my abba. Mercury Clothing." Diagonally across from us, I see a skinny man with a mustache in a shop the size of two kiosks. He is holding up a t-shirt and talking to a customer. There is nothing about him that resembles the boy next to me. Afzal is taller than him by at least five inches. Afzal's hair is brown and that man's looks black. But I don't say any of that to Afzal. I think, *Maybe it's the angle.*

"Are you going to talk to him?"

"I don't know what to say."

He keeps standing there and I'm thinking that we're starting to look a little suspicious now.

"Let's come back tomorrow when you're ready," I say to him.

Afzal kicks the wall and turns around. That day, we find two thousand rupees and a watch. We keep all of it.

I don't see Afzal all day on Wednesday. I call him and he doesn't answer. When Thursday comes and he's still not around, I get worried. I send the newspaper boy's little brother to Afzal's home to find out what's going on. He comes back and tells me Afzal has been hurt and can't walk. The timing couldn't have been worse. The only thing to do is see for myself how badly he's been injured, if he can recover by the time we have to go on the big job. The kid yells after me for the coin I had said

I would give him, and I turn around long enough to say that
I'm having to go by myself after all, aren't I?

Afzal's house is quiet. His sister has only one child, a seven-
year-old girl, and she's probably playing by the railway lines.
I rap gently on the front door, hoping that anyone but the sister
answers. It's Afzal who opens it.

I thump him on the shoulder. "You're OK! You'd scared me."

"It's just a sprain."

"So you'll be fine for next week, right?"

Afzal nods. He looks tired.

"Good. Good. You shouldn't walk around on that foot, keep
resting."

He nods again. I say goodbye and he shuts the door softly.
Still feeling light from the relief of seeing my friend able
to move, I go to the park. I manage to do four whole laps
around it.

On Fridays, my maamoo doesn't go on the fishing boat. It's
supposed to be his day of rest and prayer. On Fridays, my mami
has a list of chores for me as long as her arm. She says I don't
contribute nearly enough to the household's expenses to have
a do-nothing day. So all morning I dust the rooms, and all
afternoon I scrub the floors. Then I go to the market and buy the
things she has listed. She checks the receipt against each item
she unpacks. I know if I ask her for a break she will definitely
give me five more things to do. If I stay quiet, she might still
give me new tasks, or she might tell me to have meetha paratha
and tea.

This Friday, her mind seems to be somewhere else. I ask her what I need to do and she says, vaguely, "The floors," and disappears somewhere outside. All that running has caught up with me; I just want to lie down and take a nap. I stack up a few mattresses to make available the space I have to clean. I push the wet towel in a straight line with my foot—I'm not going to squat and pretend to care about getting the corners if Mami isn't around. I pass the slightly open door and hear the sound of crying while someone says angrily, "You cannot leave. I won't let you leave us." The angry person is my maamoo, and the crying one is my mami. I push the towel into a corner of the room, lie down on my quilt, and pull a sheet over my face.

The night before the job, I finally fall asleep around three in the morning. When I wake up the sky is bright with sunlight. It is only a little after ten; I have to find a way to kill the time before I have to go to the house. Mami sees me sitting and sends one of the children to me. "Ammi says you have to help me revise for my exam," the twelve-year-old says. Sighing, I take the Pakistan geography textbook from him. I try to get him to memorize lists of the major land features, average rainfall, and main industries of each province. At the end of almost an hour I tell him if he doesn't stop fidgeting I'll go and then he'll fail. He says he won't fail because he has never failed, and it will be a great favor to the family if I do leave. I throw his book at him and he dodges it and laughs. I swear at him and he says it doesn't matter what I call him because I'm just a charity case, an orphan, and one must make allowances for an orphan. I want to slam the main gate on my way out but I don't want Mami to get alerted.

I reach the house for the job and squat under a tree. It is too hot for anyone to be around but I want Afzal to get here fast. Five minutes later, I see him in the distance, walking slowly in the dark.

"Are you limping?" I ask. I don't try to keep the impatience out of my voice.

"It's not going to be a problem," he says, not looking at my face.

Without saying anything further, I walk around to the front. Samar Aunty would have unlocked the gate for us. In his haste to keep up with me, Afzal stumbles and a hiss escapes his mouth. I bite my lips so I don't tell him off for making our job more dangerous because of his foot problem. He manages to hobble ahead of me to the front door. It is dark inside. We take small steps forward, our eyes darting around, trying to make sense of objects unfamiliar to us. My stomach aches with worry. "Samar Aunty?" Afzal's voice is small, like a little boy's. Then he cries out; in the dark, I see him stumbling and falling. Samar Aunty is on the floor. She is not moving even though Afzal's foot has struck her.

I drop into a crouch. Her eyes are closed. Her breathing is shallow and quick. "Samar Aunty, what happened?"

On the other side of her Afzal says, "Are you hurt? Is there someone in the house?"

He moves the light from his phone screen over her body. We see blood underneath her.

"Fuck!" I breathe out. The ache in my stomach turns into nausea.

"She's not dead, she's not dead," Afzal says rapidly. He puts the phone into his pocket. "We have to move her."

He holds Samar Aunty's feet and I put my hands under her arms. He guides us toward a sofa and we lay her on it. I moan when I see the blood left behind on the floor. Samar Aunty's breathing has become quicker; her eyes remain closed.

"She's unconscious," Afzal says, but he doesn't sound like he is sure about that.

"We should put something on the wound," I manage to say.

"I don't know where she's bleeding from."

Afzal turns on his phone light again. There is nothing on her face, chest, or stomach. It is from the legs down that she seems to have been hurt. Gently, Afzal turns her away from us. Half of her qameez and shalwar are stuck to her body, their colors subsumed by the color of blood, the smell of which rises up to us. Afzal moans.

"I don't think we can do anything," he says, on the brink of crying.

"Get her some water."

While Afzal is gone, I look for a sheet to cover Samar Aunty with but I can't find anything in the room. I do not want to leave her on her own. I take the scarf from around my face and drape it over her. Afzal comes back with a glass of water and holds it to Samar Aunty's mouth. Water dribbles onto her neck. He apologizes to her and awkwardly dabs at her neck with his sleeve.

"Now we wait for Munnoo to come get us," he says. At that moment, we have no memory of why we were in that house in the first place.

We sit in the dark, listening to Samar Aunty breathing and the rush of the occasional car far away. When eleven o'clock has come and gone, I call Munnoo. He doesn't answer. I try again a few minutes later and he still doesn't pick up. My head begins to ache.

I say, "The bastard has ditched us."

"I'm going to check outside." Afzal doesn't shut the front door and the night breeze blows in. It brings with it a slight smell of leaves and flowers. In the original plan, the three of us were to slip out through the single gate and into Munnoo's car. Now, if he does turn up, Afzal and I will have to carry Samar Aunty all the way to the car—a longer, slower process that would increase the chance of all of us being seen. I cannot understand her copious bleeding, nor her inability to open her eyes.

Afzal returns, shutting the door. I look at him and he shakes his head.

"What are we going to do?" I ask him.

"I think we should get what we came here to get."

I stare at him for a moment. "OK. Yes. Let's do that."

Avoiding the congealing blood on the floor, I follow Afzal. Samar Aunty had drawn a map of the house for us; we had to learn where each room was. We climb the stairs to where the bedrooms are. From the biggest one, where Samar Aunty had said the husband and wife sleep, we pick up cash from inside a side table. Afzal tugs hard at the door of the cupboard. It flies open with a dull squeak of wood rubbing against wood. He reaches into the back and brings out three boxes. He tosses one to me. There is a pearl necklace inside. Afzal holds up a pair of gold bracelets. I'm starting to feel better already. I shake free a pillowcase and we put our boxes inside it. On the way out of the room I add a bottle of perfume and a nice-looking clock from the dressing table.

Samar Aunty had said no children live in this house.

Afzal and I collect a pair of cufflinks, a watch, more cash. There's a VCR upstairs. I put that into a second pillowcase. I keep opening drawers, poking into corners, throwing in CDs, crystal fruit decoration pieces, a few books. I find the CD player meant for the CDs. Afzal says we must go back down now. We find the study, and it is just the way Samar Aunty had described it: a shelf full of books, a floor lamp, and, on the table, two laptops sitting side by side. They are light—that means they are newer models and more expensive. My anxiety comes back as we walk toward the sofa we left Samar Aunty on. She is the same as before, breathing lightly and quickly. We say her name but she doesn't respond. This time Afzal calls Munnoo, but now the man's phone is switched off.

"We have to get out of here," I say to Afzal.

"We have to clean up the blood first."

"Are you stupid? There's no time for that."

He's not listening to me, though. He is already walking to the kitchen. I watch him come back with a sponge, a bar of soap, and a cup. "This is absolute shit, man," I say. "Get me a cloth or whatever." Afzal goes to the kitchen again and brings me a rag. But all we do is spread the stain. I get a bowl and fill it with water, and we rinse out the blood and use more soap. My arms begin to ache. I can't tell if we've made any improvement; the light from the phone isn't too good. I throw my rag into the bowl and stand up. "Afzal, I am going. You can bring Aunty or you can leave her here, that's up to you. I'm done with this madness." He gets up and dries his hands on his pants. "We can go now," he says.

We put our things outside by the gate. We go back for Samar Aunty. Afzal says he has to do one last thing. He comes back, limping and holding large, torn-up pieces of cloth.

"What the hell is that?" I ask him.

"There was blood on the sofa," he says. "We couldn't leave that behind."

I don't waste time telling him off. He stuffs the pieces into one of our makeshift bags.

There is only one way to manage everything: I carry Samar Aunty over my shoulder and Afzal carries the bags. We make our way slowly down the street, keeping to the walls of houses. The smell of urine is strong here but I don't care what we step on. I worry a stray dog might find us, but the only other living creature we see is a cat.

We reach Samar Aunty's house around three in the morning. We set her on the ground, adjust her qameez, and spread her dupatta over her. Covered in sweat, our limbs aching, Afzal and I make our way to where Munnoo lives. I am furious at him but can't think of where else to go. His gate is unlocked. We walk from the front room to the back room to his office on the other side of the curtain, but there is nobody there. We slide the bolt, tie the mouths of the bags to our wrists, and collapse into oblivion.

———

I am the first of the two of us to move into Munnoo's house.

When morning comes and I go to my mami's, her oldest son has to hold her back from beating me with the heel of her shoe for being away a whole night. While she's screaming, I quickly pick up my clothes and my comb. My cousins can use the other things if they want to. No one asks me where I'm going.

Two weeks later, Afzal and I go to Samar Aunty's house with her share of the money from the goods sold from that job. We find out she is dead. She hemorrhaged from a miscarriage, her sister tells us. "She died outside the house," her sister says, puzzled and hurt. Afzal and I take the money back with us. We do not talk on the way. Afzal goes on home, and I walk around with the extra money in my pocket. I end up buying myself shoes, a shirt, and pants.

I start getting the staff together for meetings in Munnoo's office. I install a new lock on the gate. I call Munnoo's number a few times but I always get the powered-off recording. I put crates and boxes down the middle of the front room so there is a space for Afzal and a space for me.

But Afzal doesn't want to leave his sister's place. He says he can't do this to his family. I tell him I'm like his brother and he says I don't understand. He attends all the meetings but he looks preoccupied. I think, *It's the shock from Samar Aunty's death.*

One night there is a hammering on the gate and I take out my gun in case it's Munnoo come back to claim what he had ditched. But it is a boy who lives in the street. Afzal ate a lot of medicine, he says excitedly. He's not waking up. He's in the hospital.

By the time I get there, Afzal's stomach has been pumped and he is asleep. His sister crouches in a far corner of the emergency ward, hugging her daughter and weeping, while her husband stands next to Afzal. When he sees me, he shakes his head. His eyes, like mine, are wide in pain and surprise.

When Afzal is ready to leave the hospital, his brother-in-law brings him to me, to Munnoo's house. He said Afzal's sister didn't want her daughter to be around someone who could put dangerous ideas about life and death into her head.

For a few days, I talk to Afzal about the different jobs the boys have been going on, which haven't been many. I don't ask him why he did what he did. It's only when the matter of an assignment at a watch shop in Lunda Bazaar comes up that he talks to me about it.

He'd gone to his abba and told him who he was. His abba was surprised but not unhappy. They ate a meal together. His abba said that from now on they must meet at least once a week. Afzal gave him money, the unexpected extra from Samar Aunty's death as well as most of whatever else he had saved. When he went to him again the next day, his abba wasn't there. His shop was closed. The shutter was padlocked. Afzal waited all afternoon and all evening, standing across from it. No one volunteered any information and he didn't like to ask. Around six, a wallet-seller finally told him that the Mercury Clothing man didn't work there anymore. He hadn't left any word for Afzal; no letter, no message.

Every morning, we send one of the children in the street to get our breakfast. Then we get to work. We have a team of ten people. They do what Afzal and I used to do, with minor changes: no guns, toy or real, and no women. And we don't have any women on the staff either.

Afzal doesn't talk as much as he used to; mostly he seems like his mind is somewhere else. But he eats when I tell him to, and he doesn't mind when I send someone to check on him when he's been by himself too long.

One evening my cousin Tipu, the geography test one, finds his way to my new house. He's brought us a little food from my mami: paratha and qeema. He asks me and Afzal about our work and we tell him we buy and sell used products. He says, "Right," then takes out a Pakistan Studies textbook.

"I have a test tomorrow."

"I hate your school," I say.

Tipu ignores me and turns to Afzal. "If you have some minutes, can you help?"

"Don't get into this," I say. "This kid is hopeless. Nothing stays in that brain."

Afzal takes the book. They go over and over the same facts, first one then the other: Ravi, Jhelum, Indus, Chenab, Sutlej. Jhelum comes from the Kashmir Valley and is part of Chenab; Sutlej is also called the Red River; Chenab is made by the Chandra and Bhaga rivers in the Himalayas, where Ravi also starts; Indus is the longest river in Pakistan. I close the door to the front room, muffling the sounds of their revision. This is the only time Afzal comes out of his fog and looks a little happy.

Tipu comes over almost every week. Sometimes he brings along another brother or sister. Mami always sends something for us with him. The girls, Erum and her cousin, don't come by at all. I ask Afzal if this is really the best use of having our own place, and he shrugs that he's not stopping anyone from visiting us. This is true. My cousins like it here because of how Afzal teaches them. The girls, when we asked them to stop by, had been deeply offended. "Is it really your own house?" Erum asked, skepticism in her voice. I told her yes; we ate there, we slept there, we used the bathroom there. Maybe the mention of the bathroom offended her the most.

Afterward, Afzal said I shouldn't have lied about the house.

"How is it a lie? Do we not actually live here?"

"We do, but it's Munnoo who owns it. I think. Definitely not us, though."

I let out an exasperated huff. "Well, then find out who owns it and let's buy it."

"I wouldn't feel like it's my home even if I owned it."

"So you want to live here, temporarily, forever."

Afzal says he can't talk to me when I'm like this.

This is part of his moodiness. Once, while waiting for two members to come back from a job, he asked me, "Do you want to keep doing this same thing all your life?"

"I don't mind, really," I said. "You don't?"

He shook his head. "Definitely not. I'm getting out in a month. Two, at the most."

The old anxiety started up in my stomach. I had done this work with him since we were fifteen. "What are you going to do?" I asked him.

"Teach, maybe. Or train with a mechanic. Do something clean and fair."

"My abba sold combs and hairbrushes at traffic lights. On his feet all day. Exhaust fumes in his face. He died a slow, miserable death. And my dada before that? His sorry little restaurant run to the ground because of the police. Didn't even last a year. Don't teach me about fair."

A few days after this we go to the doctor because the limp in Afzal's leg isn't going away. He doesn't want me to go with him but maybe I wear him down or maybe he is tired and in pain so he stops resisting. He tells the doctor the same thing he's told me, that it is an old sprain, but the doctor says his ankle is broken and has been so for a long time now. "How long?" I ask him. "At least four months," he answers. That was when Afzal was limping around the house, when Samar Aunty had been bleeding. I watch with my mouth dry as the doctor puts a cast around the ankle. Afzal refuses the crutches. At home, I practice in my head the right way to ask him if his sister did that to his foot, if she hit him with a brick or a stick or a rod, but I cannot make the words come to my mouth. What would we do with the words out in the open? What would we do if he lies and we both know it's a lie?

Now, if he starts a controversial topic with me, I don't argue with him. I pretend to agree.

But he keeps trying to start a fight. He says I could learn a few things from Munnoo. He says we shouldn't take my mami's food anymore. When the rest of the team comes over he prefers to stay in the other room. When he does sit with us, he stays at the back, reading. He hasn't been on a job in a long time.

I don't push him into doing what he doesn't want to do. But to try to end his moroseness I call Erum one day. I tell her Afzal is feeling a little sad, and maybe we could all just go as friends to the park or the beach to cheer him up. She says we have to stop making excuses for calling her. Then she hangs up.

I don't mind doing the extra work I have to do. I like having the people report to me and I like strategizing with them. Back when Munnoo was around, I was on the same level as some of them. I don't think they're unhappy with the situation now. I listen, take a smaller cut. Maybe living in Munnoo's house has made it easier for them to see me in his old role. Maybe having a quiet, unassuming person like Afzal around makes me look good too.

So when one of the juniors says in a meeting we could be doing a lot better if we had a girl on the staff, and most of the others agree, I don't know what to say. "I can recommend someone who's a good fit for this role," the boy tells me. Afzal is no help; he doesn't look up from my cousin's schoolbook. The others say we should try the girl out for one week, a probationary period. I give in.

She arrives on time on Saturday morning. Her name is Fiza. She is twenty-six years old and works as a cleaner the way Samar Aunty used to. "I am very good at my job," she adds. I'd never wondered why Samar Aunty did what she did; she'd always just been there, part of the whole operation. I ask the girl to explain her reason for wanting to work with us and she says, "Same as yours. Money." I tell her she can start; Afzal and I will see how it goes for a week or two. I give her the details of a small job. And then I make myself add, "If you get pregnant, you will have to stop working here. So just don't."

Fiza is efficient. In meetings, she doesn't smile unless she finds the joke especially funny, and then it is a quick one. I don't ever hear her laugh. She keeps a chadar around her all the time and prefers to stand when inside the office.

Maybe it's her unobtrusiveness as well as her skills that make her a part of us. I forget about the probation period. Money flows in steadily and Afzal seems different. He doesn't always sit at the back now, away from the rest of us, and sometimes he talks. Sometimes he even addresses Fiza.

"I think you like her," I say to him one night.

"I think you're wrong," he replies.

But I've good reason to believe what I said. I don't know when he got them but he has a few new shirts now. And I think his hair looks different. It's neater. One afternoon I see them talking in the office, sitting on chairs six feet apart, and after that they meet so often that the fact of their being together becomes a part of all three of our lives.

It is Fiza who finds Afzal the bookbinder job. It is in Paper Market. He leaves in the morning and comes back at night. This is the least money he has ever made possibly, but I don't say anything because it's the most content he has ever looked. Sometimes I tease him that he and Fiza couldn't be more different; she steals from homes she cleans, and he sits behind a table putting glue on book spines. I tell him he should marry her, no girl that exciting could accept a man that boring. He says he's thinking about it.

Only one bad thing happens in this time: Afzal's brother-in-law Saleem comes over with a message from his sister. She isn't feeling well and wants to see Afzal. I tell him not to go, she will find a way to make him unhappy. But he tells Saleem that he'll see her soon, and he tells me he has to do the right thing. The day he gets ready to go to her house, I am not able to do much. The pain from anxiety comes back to gnaw at my insides. Six hours later, when I hear the door open and see him come in, I don't know if I should punch him or hug him.

"What happened?" I ask him.

He says, "I didn't go."

It is around a week after this that a big opportunity comes the way of the business. It is at a house Fiza works for. On a Friday night in August the family will be out at a wedding. I tell Fiza I'm up for the job. Afzal, who has been listening, says he would go as well. I don't make a big deal about it while the others are around, but the moment they leave I ask him if he's lost his mind.

Fiza says, doubt in her voice, "Are you sure?"

Afzal shrugs. "I used to do this work all the time. This is my last assignment. I need an official last one."

The sky is overcast as the three of us go along the roads. I park under a tree and there is a crack of thunder just then. Getting inside the house is easy. The things we gather are few but valuable. Within an hour, we are ready to go back. We pick up the bundles and run to the car as the first drops start to come down. We slam the doors shut as I start the engine. The noise of the raindrops pelting the car is almost deafening.

I laugh from relief and shout out, "Congratulations!"

Afzal turns around to look at Fiza. "You all right?"

"Yes!"

Briefly, they hold hands. Afzal takes his phone out and looks for a song to play even though we won't be able to really hear it. Then, in the rearview mirror, I think I see a car, and I wonder if it's only my imagination. I speed blindly through the rain. There is the sound of a gunshot, tearing through the night.

ACKNOWLEDGMENTS

For the patient care they gave this book and for their guidance: Chad Luibl, Amanda Uhle, Amy Sumerton, and Cameron Finch.

For excellent insights and support, editorial and otherwise: Ahsan Butt, Beth Staples, and my Tin House 2019 people (you know who you are).

For her kindness and thoughtfulness since I first knew her in 1993: my English teacher Ms. Sawsan Imady, who wrote at the end of a 7th grade assignment, "Send me your first book."

And for being there from the start of the main thing in a hundred different incomparable ways: Ali, Shehrezad, and Zaraar.

ABOUT THE AUTHOR

FARAH ALI is from Pakistan. Her work has been anthologized in the *Pushcart Prize XLIV* and has received special mention in the 2018 Pushcart anthology. Her stories can be found in *Shenandoah*, *The Arkansas International*, *The Southern Review*, *Kenyon Review* online, *Copper Nickel*, and others.